The Confession of

Fitzwilliam Darcy

The Confession of Fitzwilliam Darcy

MARY STREET

BERKLEY BOOKS, NEW YORK

THE BERKLEY PUBLISHING GROUP
Published by the Penguin Group
Penguin Group (USA) Inc.
375 Hudson Street, New York, New York 10014, USA
Penguin Group (Canada), 90 Eglinton Avenue East, Suite 700, Toronto, Ontario M4P 2Y3, Canada
(a division of Pearson Penguin Canada Inc.)
Penguin Books Ltd., 80 Strand, London WC2R 0RL, England
Penguin Group Ireland, 25 St. Stephen's Green, Dublin 2, Ireland (a division of Penguin Books Ltd.)
Penguin Group (Australia), 250 Camberwell Road, Camberwell, Victoria 3124, Australia
(a division of Pearson Australia Group Pty. Ltd.)
Penguin Books India Pvt. Ltd., 11 Community Centre, Panchsheel Park, New Delhi—110 017, India
Penguin Group (NZ), 67 Apollo Drive, Rosedale, North Shore 0632, New Zealand
(a division of Pearson New Zealand Ltd.)
Penguin Books (South Africa) (Pty.) Ltd., 24 Sturdee Avenue, Rosebank, Johannesburg 2196, South Africa

Penguin Books Ltd., Registered Offices: 80 Strand, London WC2R 0RL, England

THE CONFESSION OF FITZWILLIAM DARCY

Published by arrangement with Robert Hale Ltd.

This is a work of fiction. Names, characters, places, and incidents either are the product of the author's imagination or are used fictitiously, and any resemblance to actual persons, living or dead, business establishments, events, or locales is entirely coincidental. The publisher does not have any control over and does not assume any responsibility for author or third-party websites or their content.

PRINTING HISTORY
Robert Hale edition / 1999
Berkley trade paperback edition / March 2008

Library of Congress Cataloging-in-Publication Data

Street, Mary.
 The confession of Fitzwilliam Darcy / Mary Street.—Berkley trade paperback ed.
  p. cm.
 A retelling of the story of Jane Austen's novel Pride and prejudice from the point of view of Mr. Darcy.
  ISBN 978-0-425-21990-4 (trade pbk.)
  1. Bennet, Elizabeth (Fictitious character)—Fiction. 2. Social classes—Fiction.
3. Poor families—Fiction. 4. Rich people—Fiction. 5. Landowners—Fiction. 6. England—
Fiction. 7. Darcy, Fitzwilliam (Fictitious character)—Fiction. I. Austen, Jane, 1775–1817.
Pride and prejudice. II. Title.

PR6069.T688C66 2008
823'.92—dc22   2007046442

PRINTED IN THE UNITED STATES OF AMERICA

10 9 8 7 6 5 4 3 2 1

The Confession of
Fitzwilliam Darcy

One

I KNOW NOT HOW MISS ELIZABETH BENNET CON-trived to bring herself so much to my notice throughout the course of that evening.

It could not have been my own doing, for I did not admire the lady and I had no wish to flatter her with any appearance of attention. Indeed, had I chosen to watch one of the Bennets it would have been her sister Jane, who far surpassed her in beauty. Yet time and time again, wherever my gaze chanced to alight, Miss Elizabeth Bennet happened to be there.

I saw her in the dance, with successive partners. I saw her talking to Sir William Lucas. Later, I saw her again in conversation with Miss Charlotte Lucas. Still later, I found myself watching her assisting Miss Maria Lucas with some adjustment to her gown.

At one point, I even found myself moving towards the lady. I stopped abruptly and turned away, determined she should have no more of my attention, whatever arts she employed.

I spent the next hour steadfastly refusing to glance in her direction: instead, I watched Bingley dancing with other ladies.

This occupation became irksome.

There I was, listening to loud, indifferent music, watching self-important strangers at their ungainly dancing, wholly indignant to find myself in such society, and out of humour with Bingley for bringing me to spend an evening here, at an unfashionable country assembly.

I am a gentleman of Quality: I am not accustomed to attending public assemblies and I had not agreed to attend this one in Meryton with any expectation of pleasure.

I was here because Bingley, with his usual impetuosity, had taken a lease on an estate at Netherfield Park: shortly after he had established himself, he invited me to stay with him.

'You must come, Darcy,' he had said. 'Now, I may repay some of the hospitality I have had from you at Pemberley. There will be some good sport, I promise you.'

He had invited his sisters, also. Our party had come from town only yesterday. Whilst he was showing me my way around the house, Bingley had confessed himself impatient to become better acquainted with his neighbours.

In every neighbourhood there were families who had daughters to be disposed of in marriage. Since Bingley and I were both single gentlemen in possession of good fortune, we could hardly escape the acquaintance of his neighbours.

I said as much. 'You may depend upon it,' I told him, 'we will be invited to sample all the delights local society has to offer without having to exert ourselves at all.'

His sisters agreed, telling me he had been visited by several of the local gentry very soon after his arrival.

Among them was a Mr Bennet who, according to Miss Bingley, had five daughters. 'And all of them unmarried.'

'In which case,' said Mrs Hurst, with a hint of malice, 'we must give him due credit for not being the first to call!'

Bingley acknowledged his sister's remarks with a faint smile. 'The Bennets are one of the principle families in the neighbourhood,' he told me. 'Their estate is at Longbourn, about three miles away. What is more,' he went on with an air of anticipation, 'I have it on good authority that the two eldest sisters are the most beautiful women in Hertfordshire. I hope to make their acquaintance tomorrow evening.'

That was when I learnt he had engaged for our party to attend a public assembly.

I was never more annoyed.

'It is fortunate indeed that you wait until we have arrived in Hertfordshire before breaking this news,' I said grimly. 'Had I known of it before I left town, I would have recalled a pressing matter of business. Bingley, how could you?'

Bingley chuckled. 'I know you do not care for dancing, Darcy, but it will do no harm to show ourselves in company. I can think of no better way to introduce ourselves in society.'

'In my opinion, you would make a better beginning by restraining yourself and showing a little reserve.'

He would not, of course. Bingley had never learnt how to repel, how to put frost between himself and others. Never did he seem to feel the necessity. He was agreeable, even to the most insufferable.

Caroline Bingley contrived to agree with both of us: she had no doubt most of the neighbours would be intolerable; attending a country assembly would be a tedious way of spending an evening. We could, however, take the opportunity to form an opinion of local society, observe our neighbours, discover who might be encouraged and determine who should not.

'Should our own judgement incline us to be too favourable to anyone,' she added with a smile, 'we shall rely upon yours, Mr Darcy, to correct us.'

'Well, the rest of you can sit in judgement and be as aloof and disdainful as you choose,' said Bingley. 'For my part, I mean to dance with every pretty girl I can find.'

Bingley was determined upon attending the assembly: spending an evening in such a way was much against my own inclinations, yet I knew that had I determined to remain at home, Miss Bingley would have chosen to keep me company.

I had reasons for avoiding a situation of that nature.

There was nothing to be done about it: I must accompany them to the Meryton assembly. I had expected to be bored. I had not expected to be so provoked by the presence of one woman.

Now, Miss Elizabeth Bennet was sitting down without a partner, not far from where I was standing.

I refused to look at her again.

Instead, I reviewed the evening from the beginning.

I had not liked the way the buzz of conversation died away as we entered the assembly rooms: I had not liked the sensation of being stared at by strangers. And, as I occupied myself in finding seats for the ladies of our party, I had very much disliked what I chanced to overhear.

'. . . Darcy . . . friend of Mr Bingley . . . from Derbyshire. . . . A single gentleman . . . vast estates. . . . Pemberley . . . yes, that Darcy. Some relation to the Fitzwilliams you know. . . . Such a handsome young man . . . ten thousand a year. . . .'

It was always the same. By some process, a whole roomful of strangers could know everything within five minutes.

I had taken some wine and stood back against the wall, regarding the assembled company without enthusiasm. From somewhere close by, I heard a clear feminine voice. 'Property, riches, and the good sense to be handsome! He must be in want of a wife!'

I stiffened, irked by this evidence that already I was an object of interest to a designing female.

Her words were answered by a soft, ladylike chuckle. 'Oh, Lizzy!'

The lady who found 'Lizzy' diverting was, I discovered, the only woman in the room who was worth a second glance. She was tall, graceful, with perfect classical features and hair the colour of ripe corn. Her eyes were blue and her mouth was smiling with a most pleasing serenity. This, unless I was very much mistaken, was one of the famous Bennet sisters.

I did not, then, trouble to look at the impertinent 'Lizzy'.

The fair beauty was enough to hold my attention for a while. She was not fashionably dressed and a closer, more critical appraisal taught me her smile was a little too wide, but she was still, without a doubt, the handsomest woman I had seen for some time.

Should she prove herself as graceful in the dance as her demeanour suggested, then here, perhaps, was one lady it would not be a disgrace to stand up with. I am not, however, a man given to flattering the ladies with any appearance of eagerness. She could wait until later.

I moved away when I saw the lady being claimed for the first dances by a lanky young man with large teeth.

It came as no surprise to see that Bingley had found himself a partner. I occupied myself by trying to discover the second beauty, sister to the first. I could not. None of the other ladies bore her any resemblance.

As I strolled around the room, a loud and rather silly female voice caught my attention. 'Stuff and nonsense! They are both very charming women and so elegant! The richness of lace on Mrs Hurst's gown. . . . I am sure they will be most agreeable neighbours. I must say I am vexed to see Mr Bingley stand up with Charlotte Lucas! However, I am persuaded he cannot admire her, at all.'

'Mama. . . .'

'We know she is a very good sort of girl, Lizzy, but you must own she is not at all handsome. Indeed, no one can think so, and I am persuaded the gentlemen . . .'

Thankfully I was, by this time, too far away to hear the

rest. I made a point, however, of taking a look at the speakers, for I had recalled the name 'Lizzy' in connection with certain remarks.

Already, I had no great opinion of her character: one glance was sufficient to inform me I had no great opinion of her person, either. She was, I judged, around twenty years old, dark-haired, tolerable, I suppose, but I would not have described her as pretty: certainly, she was no beauty.

As for her mama, she was an absolute fright of a woman with a silly, petulant expression and a discontented set to her mouth. I could hear her shrill voice above the murmur of general conversation and, although I did not catch her words, she appeared to be scolding her daughter. This might have accounted for the blank expression on that lady's countenance.

I had turned my attention to Bingley and his partner.

Plump and plain, Charlotte Lucas wore a most unbecoming shade of green. She seemed to have no illusions about her own charms, however, for her countenance bore an expression of rueful humour and, as the dance ended, I saw why. Clearly, Bingley had requested her to introduce him to the only handsome woman in the room.

He engaged that lady for the next two dances.

I engaged Mrs Hurst, for the first of my duty dances.

Somehow, she had learnt the fair beauty was indeed one of the Bennet sisters, Miss Jane Bennet, the eldest of five.

'By all reports, she is an excellent creature, with the sweetest disposition imaginable.'

I watched Bingley, dancing with the lady. He seemed satisfied with her. She moved with grace, appeared to converse easily and showed every appearance of enjoying his attentions.

With some ill humour I said, 'When a lady is endowed with superior beauty, all reports of her disposition should be received with the gravest suspicion.'

'Oh, certainly! A proper reserve is always advisable at the beginning of an acquaintance. Now, what think you of Miss Elizabeth Bennet? Her beauty is not equal to her sister's.'

'Which is she?' I asked, but I had guessed. The insufferable 'Lizzy', who had spoken of my situation with designs of her own, was sister to the fair beauty.

I looked at her again when Mrs Hurst directed my attention to her. Now, she was no longer seated and I had a better view of her. She was shorter than Jane, dark where her sister was fair: her features were very far from classical, and I would have described her figure as sturdy rather than elegant.

I pronounced myself very surprised indeed to learn that she was considered a beauty.

The movement of the dance obliged me to turn: for a time, I lost sight of the second Miss Bennet.

After dancing with Caroline Bingley, I stood back, duty done, watching Bingley being introduced to a child of no more than fourteen summers. Mrs Hurst seemed to be well informed. 'Another Lucas,' she said. 'Maria Lucas.'

Bingley engaged Maria Lucas to dance with him, possibly vexing the foolish Mrs Bennet once again.

Other Bennets were pointed out to me. I heard Miss Mary Bennet described to Miss Bingley as 'the most accomplished girl in the neighbourhood', which might have impressed had I not heard another murmur, 'Also, the most boring girl in the country.'

The two youngest Bennets, Catherine and Lydia, were pretty girls, though their manners left much to be desired. Their laughter was shrill enough to make a man wince and they seemed to spend the evening squabbling with each other, competing for partners and flinging themselves into the various dances with far more energy than grace. They had no regard for any of the other dancers and frequently caused annoyance by bumping into other people or treading on their toes.

My opinion of these two was quickly decided. They had neither dignity nor sense to recommend them, and their mother was just as bad. I hoped Bingley would not find Miss Jane Bennet too agreeable, for her relations did her no service at all.

Without meaning to, I found myself watching Miss Elizabeth Bennet as she danced. I saw she was lighter on her feet than her eldest sister, and indeed, a much better dancer.

Her partner, a stout man, did not do her justice. But she was conversing with him and seemed perfectly happy. She was smiling, which gave her countenance a more agreeable expression than the blank-faced look I had first witnessed in her. Perhaps he, too, was a man of property and riches.

It was not the first time I had found my gaze straying in her direction: I looked away, but shortly afterwards it happened again. Several times, I was obliged to wrench my gaze away and I began to comprehend that Miss Elizabeth Bennet's designing schemes were assisted by the most astonishing guile. She had some means by which she could fix my attention on herself.

I know not what manner of art she employed: never before had I known a lady who possessed such a gift. Discerning it did nothing to improve my opinion of her: it merely strengthened my resolve against her.

Determined to pay her no more attention, I turned away, seeking other diversions. But I found little amusement in watching Bingley presenting Miss Jane Bennet to his sisters, and still less in seeing the younger Bennet girls growing steadily more boisterous.

I felt myself increasing in boredom and irritability.

One elderly lady, apparently determined to make some approach, asked me how I liked Netherfield. I answered her coldly and contrived, by my manner, to make it clear I did not wish to be drawn into conversation.

Time passed: I looked at my watch, hoping we could soon take our leave.

I saw Mrs Bennet looking quite indecently triumphant and wished Bingley had more sense than to engage Miss Jane Bennet to dance with him a second time.

I stood alone, disapproving of all that I saw. Bingley was watching me and I knew I was irritating him. He came over to remonstrate with me, but by this time even he could not bring me out of my ill humour.

He insisted I should dance. I gave way to bitter complaint: he knew I did not care for dancing, assemblies such as this

were insupportable, his sisters were engaged with other partners and he was monopolizing the only handsome woman in
the room.

Bingley persisted. He wanted me to dance with one of the
fair Jane's sisters and pointed out that one of them was not far
away, sitting down without a partner.

I knew perfectly well that one of them was not far away, sitting down without a partner. I knew who she was, even though
I had kept my resolution to avoid looking at her; Miss Elizabeth Bennet had contrived to ascertain I was informed of her
whereabouts.

She should not have the satisfaction of knowing her powers
could draw me. I had not the smallest intention of partnering
that lady in the dance.

'Which do you mean?' I looked round at her, but turned
away when her eyes met mine. Something in her expression
tempted me, had me wavering. I was saved only by a surge of
resentment.

I recalled the whole of that evening: my disgust of her
mother; the vulgar behaviour of her younger sisters; the way
she herself had somehow drawn me into noticing her far more
than I wished; and the strongest recollection of all was the remark I had overheard and the way it had rankled.

Let her, I thought savagely, find out what it was like to be
obliged to overhear strangers discussing your person and situation.

Knowing she would hear, I turned to Bingley expressing
the opinion that she was tolerable, 'but not handsome enough

to tempt me'. I said I was in no humour to give consequence to young ladies who were slighted by other men. 'You had better go back to your partner and enjoy her smiles, for you are wasting your time with me.'

Bingley gave me an appalled look and stalked away. I own to a great feeling of satisfaction in having punished Miss Elizabeth Bennet. I shifted my stance so I could determine her reaction.

Had she looked at all stricken, I might have made amends. I like to think I would: I cannot say for certain. But Miss Elizabeth Bennet did not look stricken. She sat very erect, immobile, her chin neither lifted nor drooping. Her profile betrayed no expression that I could fathom.

I had witnessed that blank-faced expression earlier, on the only occasion when the smile was absent. Now, it pleased me. It convinced me that, for all her artfulness, she had little real intelligence. The girl might be quieter than her mother, but she was like her: she was just as deficient.

I turned away to get some wine and did not waste another thought on her until, with astonished indignation, I saw Bingley himself engaging Miss Elizabeth for the next dance.

I strolled back to Bingley's sisters, finding myself more in accord with them than I had for some time. We agreed it would be insupportable to spend many evenings in this way, in such company.

They told me about Jane Bennet. 'A very sweet girl,' said Mrs Hurst. 'Such pleasing manners, and they tell me her sister, Miss Eliza Bennet is a tolerable lady.'

I had something of my own to say about that.

'I fear you are not an easy man to please, Mr Darcy,' said Mrs Hurst.

'The younger girls are shockingly ill-behaved,' said Miss Bingley. 'And as for the mother! You have remarked her, Mr Darcy, I am sure. Intolerable woman!'

'Insufferable,' I agreed. 'That is one family I am not disposed to cultivate.'

'Well, I feel sorry for Jane Bennet. It is very sad she should be encumbered by such unfortunate relations.'

Having disposed of the Bennets, the sisters then went on to acquaint me with the opinions they had formed of the Lucases.

'Sir William Lucas received his knighthood at St James's Court,' said Miss Bingley. With a tremor of indignation, she added, 'He told me all about it. I am persuaded it is his favourite subject of conversation.'

'Let us hope it is not his only subject of conversation.'

'I rather think it is.'

We spent the rest of the evening in this manner, regarding the assembled company with no enthusiasm.

Bingley danced with the ladies; Miss Elizabeth Bennet danced with other gentlemen.

Eventually, the musicians began to put away their instruments. 'At last!' sighed Miss Bingley, echoing my own sentiments.

Bingley had found pleasure in the evening. He was quite put out to discover the event was drawing to a close, dismayed to discover the next assembly was not for another four weeks.

He went on to assure himself of great success with all the ladies of Hertfordshire by impetuously declaring an intention of giving a ball at Netherfield.

Caroline Bingley raised her eyes heavenward and invited me, with a look, to share her exasperation.

I might have done so, had not my attention been caught by one pair of eyes: eyes which were looking at me; eyes which held an expression of expectancy; eyes which were gleefully anticipating my displeasure.

And I knew, with a vague feeling of uneasiness, there was, after all, nothing deficient about Miss Elizabeth Bennet.

Two

─⟨⟩─

ALTHOUGH I HAD BEEN OBLIGED TO REVISE ONE OF my opinions regarding Miss Elizabeth Bennet, this did not incline me to favour that lady with greater admiration. When she came with the other Bennets to pay a morning visit, I studied her closely, determined to discover any flaws which I had overlooked at the Meryton assembly.

She had very little beauty to recommend her, and I said as much to Bingley. I insisted her features were not at all handsome, her figure lacked symmetry, her manners were by no means those of the fashionable world.

'Well, I think she is uncommonly pretty,' said Bingley defiantly. 'And from what I have seen of her so far, I would say she is most friendly and agreeable. She is not the equal of her sister, of course, but that lady is without parallel. No angel in

Heaven could be more beautiful or amiable than Miss Jane Bennet.'

I believe my friend would have quarrelled with me had I not been willing to allow that the eldest Miss Bennet was very pretty: he came near to it when I said she smiled too much.

'You should try smiling, yourself,' he said with a sudden flash of spirit. 'Do you never tire of being displeased, Darcy? Upon my soul, I believe you take pleasure in finding fault and looking at the world with disdain.'

I was taken aback, for even a hint of temper in Bingley was most unusual: as a rule, he is the most amiable of men. 'Am I so disagreeable?' I asked.

'Sometimes you are.' Then he grinned. 'You know you are.'

'Have you determined what is to be done about it?'

'There is nothing to be done about it,' he said seriously. 'You are too clever. You will descend to the level of ordinary mortals only by falling violently in love and making yourself ridiculous.'

'Heaven forbid!'

'In your case, Heaven may,' replied Bingley, 'though I confess I have not entirely given up hope.'

I regarded him searchingly, wondering if he hoped I would succumb to his sister's charms: it could not have escaped his notice that the lady was favouring me with her attentions.

I was not deceived: her design was matrimony, but I knew her affection for me had been greatly assisted by her admiration of Pemberley and by her ambition to increase her wealth and consequence.

For Bingley's sake I was patient with her, though I was careful to give her no encouragement. She was pretty, she could be good company, but there was something calculating about her which repelled any desire for greater intimacy.

It was not a subject I could discuss with her brother. I only said, 'Why should falling in love make me ridiculous? I have often seen you fall in love in a perfectly charming way.'

'You and I are not alike, my friend.'

We were not, but I was proof against flattery and since he was disposed to court the ladies and admire their charms, I would have supposed him to be more susceptible than myself.

I was cooler with the ladies, for my situation attracted the attention of designing females. There were many ladies who looked upon me as a matrimonial prize.

There were times when this was irksome, but I would not be moved by flattery: I had long since determined my own happiness could best be served by applying some rational consideration to my choice of a wife, and I had knowledge of my own requirements which had, so far, steered me away from unsuitable attachments.

I could afford to be indifferent to fortune, although it went without saying she must have impeccable connections. I knew I could be attracted by beauty; I also knew that beauty alone would not sway me: she must have robust good health. This was an important consideration, for I needed to secure a future generation and, moreover, I had no wish to be burdened with a sickly wife.

But most important of all, any lady who aspired to become

Mrs Darcy must have superior intellect, strength of character, and a disposition which was pleasing to me.

Even though my expectations were high, I did not despair of finding such a lady.

Meanwhile, I managed my estates and enjoyed all the usual sporting and social engagements of a gentleman. There were ladies who entertained hopes of influencing my feelings, but not because I had given them cause.

That evening, Bingley's sisters were discussing Miss Jane Bennet. They said again she was a sweet girl and expressed an intention of forming a better acquaintance with her.

'Miss Eliza Bennet also seems tolerable,' added Miss Bingley. 'I would not object to knowing more of that lady, what say you, Louisa?'

Mrs Hurst agreed. 'She is a great favourite with her sister, which must surely be a point in her favour.'

'Cultivating the acquaintance of any Bennet will involve us with the less desirable members of the family,' I said.

Mrs Hurst pointed out that we could hardly escape the acquaintance. 'Silly as Mrs Bennet is, she is also determined. She will impose on us, however discouraging we are. By showing our preferences, we may have less to do with the others.'

The ladies agreed they would pay a visit to Longbourn in two days' time. Bingley declared that he would accompany them.

I made no such declaration, but in the event, I also went. The uneasy feelings I had about Miss Elizabeth Bennet were, I now perceived, insufficient to convince Bingley and his sisters that the lady had nothing to recommend her. I must produce some good, solid reasoning in support of my arguments. Clearly, then, it was necessary to observe her very closely and subject her to a most critical appraisal.

With this in mind, I went to Longbourn. We were shown into the morning room and I was piqued to discover that I would not, that day, observe any fault in Miss Elizabeth Bennet. She was not there.

Miss Jane Bennet was there, as was Mrs Bennet and two of the younger girls. All the Bingleys were welcomed with warm effusion from Mrs Bennet: my own reception was civil, but cooler. I displayed my indifference and sat down with the others.

Bingley's sisters were at their most charming, complimenting Mrs Bennet on the room, the furnishings and the delightful gardens outside. They mentioned plans for alterations at Netherfield, declaring the place had been sadly neglected. Bingley smiled at Jane Bennet: Jane Bennet smiled at everyone.

Since my own design had been defeated, I left conversation to the others. I soon learned Miss Elizabeth had taken herself out for a walk. Miss Elizabeth often went out walking in the countryside.

I was surprised she was allowed to roam about alone, but said nothing. Caroline Bingley remarked on the matter. Mrs Bennet, with many silly asides, hastened to assure Miss Bingley she could not be quite easy about it herself. Mr Bennet, however, always overruled her. Lizzy was Mr Bennet's favourite. For him, she could do no wrong.

'My sister,' said Jane Bennet mildly, 'has a deep love of the countryside and her high spirits need the relief of fresh air and exercise.'

Before we left, Bingley called upon his sisters to join him in extending an invitation to the Bennets to dine with us at Netherfield.

Later, the two ladies proposed that we should invite other neighbours to make up a large party. Bingley readily agreed to this and the Lucases, the Gouldings and the Longs were engaged to dine with us on the same evening.

'We must have them sometime,' said Mrs Hurst, when her brother was not present, 'so we might as well have them all a once. Besides, Caroline and I are agreed we could not endure a whole evening with none but the Bennets. Jane Bennet is a sweet girl, and Miss Eliza is acceptable, but the family . . . !'

That dinner party was the occasion of my first meeting with Mr Bennet, a shrewd, scholarly looking man who appeared to be in his midfifties. I realized at once that he and his wife were strangely mismatched, and I wondered what had possessed him to choose such a foolish woman. I had to suppose she had once been pretty and he had been beguiled by her looks. He would not be the only man to make such a mistake.

It was not until after dinner, when the ladies had withdrawn from the table, that he paid any particular attention to me. Then he regarded me with amused, limpid eyes and said, 'You are from Derbyshire, sir, as I understand?'

I saw the thin lips twitch as I acknowledged the fact. 'The finest county in England, if my sister-in-law is to be believed,' he went on. 'She grew up in the village of Lambton, which is in the north of the county, if I am not mistaken?'

'That is so, sir. Lambton is but five miles from Pemberley.' I was sure he did not need to be told Pemberley was mine.

'Well, well. Perhaps the world is not so large as we are pleased to think.' There was a faintly satirical note in his voice and I wondered if he meant to discover whether I had some acquaintance in common with his sister-in-law.

Perhaps something warned him not to try. Instead, he asked me about the petrifying wells, about which he had heard something. 'I must confess myself sceptical,' he said. 'I cannot really believe objects can be turned to stone, simply by placing them in the water.'

'The explanation is perfectly simple,' I told him. 'There are mineral deposits in the water which are left behind on any object placed under the spring. In time, a crust is formed. Anything so covered has an appearance of being turned to stone.'

'Ah, now I understand. You have a very succinct way of explaining matters, Mr Darcy.'

'I have that reputation, sir.'

The subject had caught Bingley's interest. 'This is incredible, Darcy,' he said. 'Never until this moment have I heard of petrifying wells, for all the times I have been in Derbyshire. Such curiosities! Why have you never spoken of them, why have you never shown them to us?'

'I had no thought of it,' I confessed. 'But since you are interested, we may visit the one in Matlock when next we go into the county.'

The rest of that dinner party was unremarkable, for my design of observing the faults of Miss Elizabeth Bennet was frustrated by the lady contriving to remain elusive. At dinner she had been seated some distance from me, where I could neither see nor hear her. Later, when we gentlemen joined the ladies in the drawing-room, my attention was claimed by Miss Bingley. Miss Jane Bennet was with that lady, but her sister was across the room, conversing with Miss Charlotte Lucas. After coffee, the card tables were brought out. Miss Elizabeth Bennet not only chose a table on the far side of the room from myself, but also seated herself where others obstructed my view of her.

That evening, I discerned nothing to support my arguments against Elizabeth Bennet and I could only repeat my assertions that she was certainly no beauty.

In spite of my assertions, the pleasing manners of the two eldest Bennet girls had grown on the goodwill of Miss Bingley and Mrs Hurst.

I was all astonishment when, dining at Longbourn a few days later, I realized that Bingley's sisters were making little progress in their overtures towards the second Miss Bennet. Miss Jane Bennet seemed pleased with their attention. Miss Elizabeth Bennet treated them with every civility but, when manners allowed her a choice of society, she showed a preference for her friend, Charlotte Lucas.

At Longbourn that evening, I discovered Mrs Bennet had a sister. Mrs Philips was a vulgar, talkative woman and the only pleasing thing about her was that she made no attempt to converse with me. She lived in Meryton and from there she had brought news which attracted the lively attention of her youngest nieces.

'A whole regiment of soldiers!' Miss Lydia Bennet could not contain her delight upon learning that a certain troop of the militia were to take up winter quarters in Meryton. 'Now we shall see some fun!'

Miss Catherine Bennet shared her sister's sentiments. Then I heard the lofty voice of Miss Mary Bennet. 'Such matters, I am afraid, have little interest for me. I much prefer a book!'

The two younger girls stared at their sister in amazement and behind me I heard a faint gurgle of laughter. I turned, and accidentally met a pair of eyes that were brimming over with merriment.

I looked away, startled by the discovery that Bingley had been right. Miss Elizabeth Bennet was indeed uncommonly pretty: in fact, the huge dark eyes with their intelligent expression gave her a quality which went beyond mere beauty.

I made certain, that evening, of positioning myself where I could observe her: my first glances discovered a flawless complexion and a healthy sheen upon the dark hair. Later, I was forced to acknowledge that, even though she lacked the elegant proportions of her sister Jane, her figure was light and pleasing.

My attention was drawn to her playful spirits when I heard her own comment on the expected arrival of the regiment. 'Indeed, I shall be most disappointed have I not had my heart broken by Christmas.'

'Oh, Lizzy!' Jane's answering chuckle brought to mind the

first time I had heard it, at the Meryton assembly. The remark which I had then found offensive was, in fact, no more than a light-hearted pleasantry, not meant to be taken seriously.

I felt a pang of regret at having refused to dance with Miss Elizabeth Bennet.

On the way back to Netherfield, Bingley's sisters were scathing in their derision of Mrs Philips, Mrs Bennet and the younger girls. 'Upon my soul,' said Mrs Hurst, 'should the officers of the regiment know what awaits them, I believe they would prefer to be fighting the French!'

Eventually, Bingley contrived to turn the conversation to the sweet girl, for whom the ladies had nothing but admiration.

I said nothing. My mind was agreeably taken up with a girl who, I suspected, was not so sweet, but who showed promise of something more interesting. I was now wishful of knowing her better.

I saw her next at a party given by Sir William Lucas. By this time, the militia had arrived in Meryton and one might have been excused for thinking they had taken up their quarters in the Lucas drawing-room, that evening. Certainly there was a liberal splash of scarlet among the more sober colours of the non-military gentlemen.

Our host and hostess were talking to the colonel of the regiment, a man named Forster, and when we went across to pay our compliments, we were introduced. Also in the group were Miss Charlotte Lucas, Miss Elizabeth Bennet and Miss Jane Bennet. Some minutes were spent whilst the others had the kind of meaningless conversation which seems necessary between strangers. I looked at Elizabeth Bennet.

Sir William and Lady Lucas moved away to greet some new arrivals, Bingley and his sisters moved away with the sweet girl. Elizabeth glanced at me, a glint of laughter in her eyes, and, as she turned to Colonel Forster, she said, 'I hope, sir, you will allow your officers to attend our Meryton assemblies. They will be greatly appreciated, I assure you. We young ladies love to dance, is that not so, Charlotte? Yet lately, there has been a most regrettable shortage of partners.'

I did not need to see the faint trace of alarm on Miss Lucas's face to know that Miss Elizabeth Bennet was taking a playful rap at me.

Colonel Forster suspected nothing. He responded with heavy gallantry. 'If that is so, ma'am, I shall insist they attend.'

Laughter gurgled in her throat. 'Thank you, you are very good. And perhaps when you are settled here, you might even give a ball yourself, sir?'

'Nothing would give me greater pleasure, ma'am, I assure you.'

Miss Elizabeth Bennet allowed herself another laughing glance at me. I could only stand, speechless, in admiration.

The ladies excused themselves, leaving me to discuss the affairs of the nation with Colonel Forster. And I, well aware it would be unwise to show my interest in Elizabeth too openly, allowed an hour to pass before I approached her again.

She had spoken to many but now she was back with Miss

Lucas. On observing my approach, the girls spoke to each other briefly, then Elizabeth, eyes sparkling, turned to me. 'Do you not think, Mr Darcy, that I expressed myself uncommonly well just now, when teasing Colonel Forster to give us a ball at Meryton?'

'With great energy.' We were not to forget the subject of balls, I surmised. Miss Bennet intended to enjoy several chuckles at Mr Darcy's expense. 'It is a subject which always makes a lady energetic.'

'You are severe on us.'

Miss Lucas seemed to feel I needed rescuing from Elizabeth's pleasantry. She nodded to me and said, 'It will be her turn soon to be teased. I am going to open the instrument, Eliza, and you know what follows.'

'You are a strange creature by way of a friend! If my vanity had taken a musical turn, you would be invaluable, but as it is . . .'

She had judged, correctly, that myself and Bingley and his sisters were accustomed to hearing some very fine musicians, a matter which brought on her own reluctance to perform.

Miss Lucas entreated, others joined in, all of them showing an expectation of pleasure when she yielded and sat down at the pianoforte.

Her performance was pleasing. She had not that degree of accomplishment which my sister, Georgiana, had attained, nor did she attempt any of the intricate pieces I had so frequently heard when Miss Bingley and Mrs Hurst sat down to play. Yet she brought an additional quality to the performance, a musical expression which went beyond accomplishment. Elizabeth was not playing for the sake of exhibiting her virtuosity: she played for joy.

I abandoned thought and listened with pleasure as she sang until her glance happened in my direction jolting me out of my reverie. Some feeling had kicked under my rib cage and I turned away, shaken and astonished at my own involuntary response.

Something was happening to me: it had been happening, I now realized, ever since I had first seen Miss Elizabeth Bennet, and I was not pleased to discover it. I had no wish to find myself becoming attached to a lady, however pleasant, whose family would attract such derision and repugnance.

There was some consolation, I supposed, in my early awareness of it, for I knew I was master of myself: I could deal with any unwelcome emotions by the power of reason.

My reason was assisted when Elizabeth was succeeded at the instrument by her sister Mary, a young lady who was always far too eager to display her own accomplishment, and did so with an air of consequence which did not become her. She played a heavy concerto, not at all suitable for a neighbourly party and, perhaps realizing it had not been well received, later gave in to the entreaties of the younger Bennets to play airs to which they could dance.

I watched in indignation as Lydia and Catherine Bennet actually dragged some of the officers into a noisy, untidy set. Some of the younger Lucases joined the dancing. I was standing near them and since conversation was now impossible, I continued my reflections on my own instinctive reactions to Miss Elizabeth Bennet.

I felt I had had been fortunate indeed to discover my own inclination before it had progressed to love. I now resolved to keep my admiration in check.

Engrossed in my thoughts, I had not noticed the approach of Sir William Lucas until he spoke. He began with an observation on the dancing, and progressed with a compliment on my own prowess in the art. Then, without the least encouragement from me, he began to talk about the dancing at St James's Court.

I had known he would: Sir William always turned the conversation to that subject. I made but short answer, hoping he would go away.

He did not. He was struck by a notion of gallantry. Having seen Elizabeth passing by, he halted her, asked why she was not dancing, took her hand and presented her to me as a very desirable partner.

'You cannot refuse to dance, I am sure, when so much beauty is before you.'

I was astonished, not only by Sir William's action but also by my own involuntary reaching for her hand. But Elizabeth, perhaps because she had been teasing me on the subject of dancing, was now thoroughly disconcerted.

She drew back. 'Indeed, sir, I have not the least intention of dancing. I entreat you not to suppose that I moved this way in order to beg for a partner.'

Looking down into her discomposed face, I knew I could

not refuse her again. Little as I relished the idea of joining that ungainly group of dancers, I begged her to allow me the honour of her hand.

She thanked me but refused and Sir William's attempt to persuade her had no effect. After a few moments she excused herself and turned away.

Thus it was that Miss Elizabeth Bennet had the distinction of being the first woman ever to refuse to dance with me.

Far from being offended, I was, on the contrary, rather pleased with her for, had she accepted, she would have obliged me to join that noisy, untidy set and exhibit myself in a manner which would have afforded the most acute embarrassment.

I watched her across the room in animated conversation with her father. Given a sufficiently grand occasion, I reflected, it would be agreeable to dance with Elizabeth. I recalled how Bingley had made a promise of holding a ball at Netherfield, and allowed myself to fall into a reverie on the subject.

This time, my musings were interrupted by Miss Bingley. She said she knew exactly what I was thinking. 'You are considering how insupportable it would be to spend many evenings in such society, and indeed, I am quite of your opinion.'

Miss Bingley was always telling me my own opinion — and affecting to share it. Now, I told her she was totally wrong in her conjecture. I told her I had been admiring the fine eyes of a lady and, upon her enquiry, I admitted the identity of the lady in question.

It startled her. 'Miss Elizabeth Bennet? How long has she been such a favourite? And pray, when am I to wish you joy?'

I had known she would wish me joy and I said so.

'I shall consider the matter as settled,' she announced. 'You will have a charming mother-in-law indeed.'

Thus she began the first of many attempts to provoke me into disliking Elizabeth by exercising her derisive wit on the subject of all my future relations.

Three

———

MY BRIEFLY EXPRESSED ADMIRATION OF MISS ELIZA-
beth Bennet had alerted Miss Bingley to the possibility of a
rival for my affection. At breakfast the next day, I discovered
she had enlisted the help of her sister. Mrs Hurst, no less than
Miss Bingley, wished me to connect myself elsewhere.

All their liking had been done away with at a stroke. They
commented disparagingly on Elizabeth's appearance; her manners, which had previously been pleasing to them, were now
considered impertinent and her performance on the pianoforte, which I had enjoyed, was slighted by these ladies who
had achieved a higher standard of virtuosity at the expense of
musical expression.

'Really, I cannot think her playing was at all remarkable,'
said Mrs Hurst. 'I cannot understand why it was so well re-

ceived. But, of course, country people rarely have the opportunity of hearing more polished performers.'

'Then you two ladies must exert yourselves to educate their taste,' I said smoothly.

The conversation was halted by Mr Hurst joining us, surly because his horse had thrown out a splint. The subject was allowed to drop, to my relief, and horses became the new topic of conversation.

In admitting admiration for Elizabeth, I had hoped to discourage Miss Bingley's ambitions by implying that her own exertions were having no effect, that she was wasting her time.

She had judged differently: in the days that followed, she paid me even more attention. Clearly, she thought the prize was worthy of greater effort.

Mrs Hurst, meanwhile, attacked Elizabeth's weakest point. The defects of her relations were often mentioned. Jane Bennet continued to be a sweet girl, but I was hearing too much about their mother's vulgarity, and already there was gossip in the neighbourhood about the flirtatious behaviour of the younger sisters with the officers of the regiment.

Miss Bingley and Mrs Hurst might have spared themselves the trouble of recounting all this gossip to me, for I had very quickly formed my own opinion of the Bennets: none save the two eldest girls seemed to have any notion of propriety, and this was quite enough to repel any thought of connecting myself with them. Though I admired Elizabeth, I did not mean to fall in love with her: I did not consider her a suitable bride.

On Tuesday, Bingley, Hurst and myself were invited by

Colonel Forster to dine in the officers' mess. It was a day of frequent heavy showers and, upon our return to Netherfield, we discovered events had taken a most unexpected turn.

Miss Jane Bennet was with the ladies, and she was feeling unwell. 'A consequence, I suppose, of my getting wet through on the way here,' she said.

She had been invited to dine with the ladies and had made the journey on horseback. Now it was raining again: clearly she could not be sent home.

Bingley, in an agony of solicitude, demanded warming pans for her bed, hot cabbage leaves to place on her sore throat, and the immediate attendance of a doctor.

'No, no, I thank you. Please, do not be alarmed on my account. I am sure I shall be well again in the morning.'

Miss Bingley ordered her maid to attend Miss Bennet and the lady, having expressed gratitude for their kindness, retired for the night.

The morning produced no improvement. A note was sent to her family and Bingley sent a servant to summon the apothecary.

Before the apothecary came, we were surprised by another visitor. Miss Elizabeth Bennet, flushed with exercise, muddied and bedraggled, had walked the three miles from Longbourn to enquire after her sister.

The ladies received her politely, incredulous as they were at her having walked so far in such dirty weather. I, myself, doubted the circumstances had justified her coming, though I could not help but admire her. The exercise had given greater brilliancy to her eyes, her complexion was heightened, and if Bingley's sisters were scandalized by the mud on her petticoat, it did her no injury with me.

'It shows an affection for her sister that is very pleasing,' said Bingley reprovingly, when his sisters' derision was at its height. I agreed with him, although I did not say so. I was persuaded Elizabeth understood the ladies and cared nothing for their opinion.

We gentlemen had an engagement to join a shooting party and I had expected Elizabeth to be gone before our return to the house. She was not, for during the day her sister had become feverish. Since the invalid could not bear to be parted from Elizabeth, Miss Bingley had, reluctantly, I suspect, invited her to remain at Netherfield.

The Bennet sisters stayed four days and, during that time, I discovered too much for my peace of mind.

Miss Bingley and Mrs Hurst had learnt more about the Bennet family and their relations. Indeed, I realized this had been their design in inviting Miss Jane Bennet to dinner. They had quizzed her on the subject and now they relayed their information to me without scruple.

I noted their unkindness, but I could not help noting their information, also. It was worse than I thought, for although Mr Bennet was a gentleman, he had married beneath him. Mrs Bennet's sister, Mrs Philips, was the wife of a country attorney who practised in Meryton. Even worse, they had a brother who was in trade and lived in Cheapside.

If the repugnance I felt for Elizabeth's closest family was

not enough, the knowledge of such low connections must strengthen my resolve to keep my admiration under control.

That first evening, our enquiries after Jane Bennet met with no favourable response. At dinner, Bingley was considerate towards Elizabeth, but his sisters ignored her and directed their attention to me, giving me little chance to look at her and none to speak.

I was vexed at being included in their incivility. When Elizabeth had returned to her sister, I contrived to turn their conversation to some of our more notable acquaintances in London. This was not difficult, for Bingley's sisters liked to associate with people of rank and it gave me the opportunity I wanted.

'Such people cannot be blamed for doubting the sincerity of those who fawn upon them whilst slighting those of lesser consequence,' I said.

I kept my eyes on the cards, for it was my turn to deal, and I avoided any suggestion of directing reproof at them. I knew my words would have the desired effect, for the sisters always made a point of agreeing with me. 'Oh, certainly! Such conduct cannot but be noticed!'

Elizabeth herself, quite unwittingly, undid all my good work. She came downstairs after her sister had fallen asleep, and the conversation somehow turned upon those attributes a lady should possess to be considered accomplished.

I had been about to express my own ideas, but Miss Bingley forestalled me: she declared a woman could not be considered truly accomplished unless she had a thorough knowledge of music, singing, drawing, dancing and the modern languages.

'And besides all this,' she went on, 'she must possess something in her air and manner of walking, the tone of her voice, her address and expressions.'

Miss Bingley had been reciting those recommendations which she believed she herself possessed.

Knowing Miss Bingley rarely read anything other than fashion journals, I said, 'She should also add something substantial to the improvement of her mind by extensive reading.' I saw my words register and wondered how soon I was to have the privilege of seeing that lady with a book in her hand.

Elizabeth, who had been reading, now set aside her book. 'I never saw such a woman,' she declared. 'I never saw such capacity, and taste and application and elegance such as you describe united.'

This innocent wisdom did not endear Elizabeth to Miss Bingley, who began abusing her as soon as she had excused herself to check on her sister.

I now wished I had left my admiration unspoken, for by expressing it I had done Elizabeth no service with Miss Bingley.

Elizabeth came downstairs only to tell us that Jane was worse and she could not leave her.

I saw real anxiety. I remained silent, wishing I could suggest some remedy. Bingley said he would send immediately for the apothecary, whilst the ladies said we should send an express to fetch one of the London physicians.

'I thank you, but no,' she said to this. 'I know my sister,' she added, with a smile that robbed her refusal of any offence, 'and I will spend the night in her room in case she needs me. Perhaps we may send for the apothecary again should there be no improvement by morning.'

'You may be certain I will,' said Bingley. Elizabeth thanked him and left. Bingley instructed his housekeeper to attend to the needs of the sick lady. I spent the rest of the evening willing Jane Bennet to recover, if only for her sister's sake.

Happily, there was an improvement by morning. The lady was by no means recovered and remained in her room, but we were thankful to hear she was beginning to mend.

That morning, Mrs Bennet came to see how her sick daughter did. She brought her younger daughters with her and the visit confirmed me in all my worst opinions of them.

Mrs Bennet was obvious, silly and shrill. She expressed opinions which she contradicted moments later, flattered Bingley and his sisters with excessive regard, snubbed Elizabeth in front of everyone and took vehement exception to some remark of mine.

Bingley's sisters were smirking in a way that I felt was almost as reprehensible as Mrs Bennet's conduct. Bingley kept his countenance and contrived to make agreeable conversation, but my own exertions seemed to excite Mrs Bennet to greater nonsense.

The two younger girls spent the visit whispering to each other. When their mother was ready to leave, one of them put herself forward in the most unbecoming way, reminding Bingley of his promise to hold a ball at Netherfield.

'When your sister is recovered, you shall name the day of the ball. You would not wish to be dancing while she is ill.'

Lydia Bennet agreed it would be better to wait until Jane was well because by that time Captain Carter would most likely be at Meryton again. 'And when you have given your ball, I shall tell Colonel Forster it will be quite a shame if he does not give one, too.'

They then took their leave, leaving me with the impression that the prospect of a ball was of greater importance to all three of them than the safe recovery of Miss Jane Bennet.

Throughout the visit, Elizabeth had been blushing for her relations. Now, she returned to her sister, and I did not see her again until dinner-time.

Mrs Bennet's visit reminded me, most forcibly, that I must not let admiration for Elizabeth get the better of me.

That evening, I chose an occupation which would allow me to ignore her without incivility. I seated myself at the escritoire, saying I must write to my sister, Georgiana.

Miss Bingley was even more teasing than usual. She seated herself beside me, remarking on the evenness of my hand, the length of my letter, desiring me to pass on her own messages to Georgiana and offering to mend my pen. Her attempts to distract me did not succeed: I continued writing.

I could not accuse Elizabeth of attempting to distract me: she was engaged with some needlework and spoke hardly at all.

Then, with the design of impressing her, Bingley began to show off and he did so in a way that vexed me, by holding up to ridicule my meticulous style of writing.

He went on to make a virtue of his own carelessness. 'My ideas flow so rapidly I have not time to express them — by which means my letters sometimes convey no ideas at all.'

'Your humility, Mr Bingley,' said Elizabeth, 'must disarm reproof.'

Indignant because he had drawn from Elizabeth a compliment which, I thought, was wholly undeserved, I turned to her, determined to set the matter right. I said his appearance of humility was deceitful and was, in fact, an indirect boast.

'You are proud of your defects in writing,' I told Bingley. 'Because it comes from rapidity of thought, you think it highly interesting. But the power of doing anything quickly without any attention to the imperfection of the performance is not estimable.'

I thought my good, solid reasoning and sound common sense deserved a better response from the lady than the half smile it received.

I continued with my theme, recalling how, only that morning, Bingley had boasted of his own precipitance. 'Whatever I do is done in a hurry,' he had said, 'and therefore if I should resolve to quit Netherfield, I should probably be off in five minutes.'

He had been speaking to Mrs Bennet, but now I suspected he had aimed the remark at Elizabeth. He meant it as a compliment to himself, his design had been to display himself as a man of swift action and strong resolution.

Had he made such a boast before any other lady, I might have let it pass. Bingley has many amiable qualities, but strength of resolution is not one of them. Of all the men I know, he is the most likely to yield to persuasion.

I said so. 'If a friend were to say, "Bingley, you had better stay till next week", you would probably do it, you would probably not go—and at another word, might stay a month.'

'You have only proved by this,' said Elizabeth, 'that Mr Bingley did not do justice to his own disposition. You have shown him off now much more than he did himself.'

Bingley, confound him, gave a triumphant smirk. But he had the grace to admit it was not what I meant. 'Darcy would think the better of me, if under such a circumstance, I were to give a flat denial and ride off as fast as I could.'

'Would Mr Darcy then consider the rashness of your original intention as atoned for by your obstinacy in adhering to it?'

'Upon my word, I cannot exactly explain the matter. Darcy must speak for himself.'

I smiled at Bingley's perplexity: the liveliness of her mind was too much for him. He had withdrawn, and now I was free to engage Elizabeth in an interesting discussion.

I reminded her that Bingley's hypothetical friend had merely asked him to stay without offering any argument in favour of doing so.

'To yield readily—easily—to the persuasion of a friend is no merit with you?'

'To yield without conviction,' I pronounced, 'is no compliment to the understanding of either.'

She raised her brows and suggested that affection between friends might be enough to persuade one to alter a decision of no great moment, without waiting to be argued into it.

I was pleased, though I could not say exactly why. I saw that Elizabeth could be a formidable opponent in any debate.

I suggested we should arrange the points of discussion with more precision. 'We should determine the degree of importance which is to appertain to this request, as well as the degree of intimacy between the parties.'

I had forgotten Bingley and his determination to show off: now he swept away all hope of continuing the discussion.

'By all means,' he cried, 'let us hear all the particulars, not forgetting their comparative height and size, for that will have more weight in the argument, Miss Bennet, than you are aware of. I assure you that if Darcy were not such a great tall fellow in comparison with myself, I should not pay him half so much deference. I declare, I do not know a more awful object than Darcy, on particular occasions, and in particular places; at his own house especially, and of a Sunday evening, when he has nothing to do.'

Clearly, Bingley felt the lady was paying too much attention to me and not enough to himself, though why he found it necessary to hold me up to ridicule, I know not. It was not his usual way and I found it particularly offensive that he should do so in front of Elizabeth.

I smiled, of course: there was nothing else to be done, and I was a little consoled because he had not succeeded in making Elizabeth laugh at me.

'I see your design, Bingley,' I said. 'You dislike an argument and want to silence this.'

'Arguments are too much like disputes. If you will defer yours till I am out of the room, I shall be very thankful.'

'What you ask,' said Elizabeth politely, 'is no great sacrifice on my side.' She resumed her needlework and smiled at me. 'Mr Darcy had much better finish his letter.'

I turned away in some dissatisfaction. Later, upon reading through my finished letter, I found I had told Georgiana a great deal about the fine eyes, the playful manners and the lively disposition of Miss Elizabeth Bennet.

I abandoned my thought of altering it when Miss Bingley drew near again. Unwilling to let her see what I had written, I folded the sheets and wrote the address.

A little later, Miss Bingley seated herself at the pianoforte. When she struck up a Scottish air, I astonished myself by approaching Elizabeth, asking if she would care to dance a reel.

Receiving no answer, I was obliged to repeat the question, and she said, 'You wish me to say "Yes" so that you might have the pleasure of despising my taste: but I always delight in overthrowing those kind of schemes. I have made up my mind to tell you I do not want to dance a reel at all. Now, despise me if you dare.'

Perhaps her refusal was to avoid giving offence to Miss Bingley, or perhaps she was still teasing me about my ill-humour at the Meryton ball. Bewitched by the laughter in her eyes, I could not be affronted. By way of making some amends for that occasion, I smiled and bowed. 'Indeed, I do not dare.'

Later, after we had retired for the night, I realized I was being less successful than I wanted to be in disguising my admiration for Miss Elizabeth Bennet. Whilst she remained at Netherfield, I found I enjoyed her society too much: I wanted more of it.

I was accustomed to ladies such as Miss Bingley, who were always exerting themselves to please, and I was very sensible that Elizabeth made no such exertions. Yet, in spite of my resolve to ignore her, she had, this evening, drawn from me more attention than I had paid Miss Bingley in a month.

I knew I looked at her more than I should. And whether I looked at her or not, I had a heightened awareness of her presence. My ears caught every slight sound of movement: the briefest glance could give me a world of information as to her appearance and her mood.

My own knowledge that any alliance with Elizabeth was impossible, frequently received quite unwanted assistance from Miss Bingley. She would taunt me about my supposed marriage. 'I hope you will give your mother-in-law a few hints as to the advantage of holding her tongue: and if you can compass it, do cure the younger girls of running after the officers.'

Unwilling to give her the satisfaction of seeing how her remarks rankled, I kept my temper and displayed only indifference, but Miss Bingley did herself no service with me, neither did she succeed in her design of provoking me into dislike of Elizabeth.

Miss Jane Bennet was sufficiently recovered to join us downstairs the next evening. Bingley was overjoyed: he spent some time ensuring her comfort and spent the rest of the evening talking to her.

I took up a book, and might have resisted all Miss Bingley's attempts to distract me, had she not drawn Elizabeth into her scheme. Then I was alert, for all her previous incivility to our guest had me suspecting a design to discompose Elizabeth.

I was mistaken: Miss Bingley simply meant to engage my attention by any means she could. But, before I knew it, I was drawn, first into an airy, insubstantial conversation which later turned into another confrontation between myself and Elizabeth.

'I am perfectly convinced that Mr Darcy has no defect,' said Elizabeth. 'He owns it himself, without disguise.'

That was just her own style of pleasantry, of course: she knew I had made no such pretension, and I would have done better to return some light answer. But there was something challenging about Elizabeth that evening, and under her coolly smiling gaze I found myself confessing to an unyielding temper and a resentment that could rarely be appeased. 'My good opinion, once lost, is lost for ever.'

'Then your defect is a propensity to hate everybody.'

Nonsensical girl! But I could only approve her design, which was to lighten a discussion which had quickly become too serious.

'And yours,' I said, smiling, 'is to wilfully misunderstand!'

Miss Bingley interrupted the discussion, suggesting music, and I, recollecting myself, was not sorry for it.

I was becoming perturbed: I am not a man who cares to

bare his soul for others, and I regretted, now, that I had said as much as I had to Elizabeth.

I was forced to acknowledge that her power was increasing. Had she sprung from a more distinguished family, my growing feelings for her might have been agreeable: as it was, I felt obliged to struggle against them.

Aware of the danger, I was relieved when, on Saturday, Jane Bennet declared herself well enough to return home. Polite protests were made, enough to persuade her to remain another day, but beyond that she would not be moved. They were to leave on Sunday, after matins.

A swift review of all that had occurred these last few days concerned me in case Elizabeth was entertaining her own hopes and expectations. I knew she understood Miss Bingley had designs on me; I thought she was quick enough to suspect jealousy in that lady's incivility to herself. And my own attentions must have betrayed my admiration for her.

I must now make it clear I had no intentions. It pained me to do so, but it was necessary.

In consequence, I hardly spoke to her on Saturday. When left alone with her, I ignored her and kept my eyes on my book, though I confess I turned over more pages than I read.

They left on Sunday, as arranged. On departure, Elizabeth seemed to be in the best of spirits. Had she been disappointed by my coolness, she gave no sign of being unhappy about it.

It would have been more gracious of me were I pleased to see her taking such a sensible attitude, but I confess I was not. I prided myself on my sense and judgement, yet here my sentiments were far from being sensible. I was mortified to discover she had more self-command than I did.

I took myself off for a walk, reminding myself of all the arguments against entertaining any design on Elizabeth Bennet. Reminding myself of the evils of such an alliance might strengthen my resolve, but there seemed to be little I could do to repress the feelings I had for Elizabeth. She was lively, and she was intelligent, and she was kind and she was lovely. I found such delight in her.

I now resolved to leave Netherfield as soon as I could. Here, I could hardly avoid seeing her and my knowledge of her and my feelings for her had grown too rapidly: should I see her often, I would be lost to every rational consideration.

At dinner, before I could make my excuses, I found Bingley had remembered his declared intention of holding a ball.

'It would not be advisable to hold it this week,' he said, 'for I am by no means persuaded Miss Bennet is fully recovered from her illness. I propose we hold it next Tuesday sennight. What say you, Darcy?'

'You cannot expect Mr Darcy to enter into your scheme with enthusiasm, Charles,' Miss Bingley reproved him. 'For him, a ball would be rather a punishment than a pleasure.'

Having determined my sentiments, Miss Bingley also affected to share them. She could hardly have been more mistaken: I was recalling how once I had promised myself the pleasure of dancing with one particular lady.

No harm would be done by putting off my excuses and departure until after the ball. No harm would be done by allowing myself one small indulgence, one dance with Elizabeth.

In spite of Miss Bingley's efforts to be entertaining, the evenings without Elizabeth had lost much of their savour and when, during the week, Bingley suggested riding to Longbourn to enquire after the health of Miss Jane Bennet, I agreed to accompany him.

We did not go all the way, for passing through Meryton we came across all the Bennet sisters in the street, talking with a group of gentlemen.

Bingley went towards them and began the usual civilities and I, in my determination not to look at Elizabeth, found myself looking at someone very different: someone I recognized.

I felt the blood drain from my face.

George Wickham!

There he was, impudent as ever, the one man I had believed I would never meet again in the whole course of my life.

There he was, the companion of my youth, the acknowledged favourite of my father, the bane of my life.

He was deep in conversation with Miss Elizabeth Bennet.

Four

‿‿

'**D**O NOT DARE TELL ME YOU ARE IN LOVE WITH SUCH
a man,' I said savagely. My sister was alarmed to see me so angry, but on that dreadful day in Ramsgate last July, I was too
intent on venting my own feelings to have much concern for
hers. 'He is a libertine, a gamester and a drunkard,' I went on
remorselessly. 'He is extravagant, false and deceitful. He has
no integrity and no conscience.'

'No!' cried Georgiana. 'This cannot be! How can you speak
of him so, sir? You know how Papa valued him.'

'I do, indeed,' I said drily. I struggled for composure, for I could
not wholly blame my sister who, in her youth and innocence, had
trusted our father's good opinion. 'He was taken in, Georgiana,
and you know not how it pained me to see it. But you shall know
the truth: I will not have Wickham insinuate himself with you.'

'I know he is not well connected,' said Georgiana tearfully. 'I thought you might object on that account, but—'

'And so I would, especially for a girl of your tender years! But I have other reasons: you deserve a better man than Wickham, my dear. He is wholly profligate.'

'There must be some mistake!' she said desperately. 'I cannot believe he is all the things you say! I remember how kind he was to me when I was small.'

'That is true,' I acknowledged. 'I can well understand that your fond memories assist your belief in him. Always he was charming, that I know. But you have been deceived by it, Georgiana. You know not what wickedness that charm conceals.'

'Oh, this is insupportable!' cried Georgiana. 'You are determined, are you not, to set me against him?'

'You may be sure I am,' I replied. 'You are a lady of good fortune, Georgiana, and fortune is Wickham's design, believe me. But I do not understand what he means to do. He knows he cannot marry you without the consent of your guardians: and he must know that neither I nor our cousin Fitzwilliam would ever give it.'

Something in the stiffening of my sister's slight figure opened up another idea on the matter. 'Oh, no! Georgiana, you cannot be planning to elope with him?'

'I had hoped I would not have to,' she cried. 'I hoped you would be reasonable and give your consent so we could be married properly.'

'An elopement!' I said in disgust. 'And you let him persuade you to this? Have you no pride, have you no regard for your own credit?'

'I wanted to be married properly,' she repeated. 'You must know I would not wish to grieve you. But he thought it was the only way we could be together.'

'I am sure he did,' I said drily. She made no answer and once again I found myself struggling to contain my feelings. 'Georgiana, you are but fifteen years old: you have lately finished school and you know but little of the world. You may believe there are many, besides Wickham, who will love you for your fortune. You need time to learn how to judge men.'

'I trusted Papa's good opinion,' said Georgiana, sulkily. 'And I do not yet understand why I should not.'

'I should think the mere fact Wickham tried to persuade you to an elopement was reason enough,' I told her. 'You may take it from me, my dear, that no man of any honour would make such an attempt.'

'But we love each other!' cried Georgiana. 'Why can you not understand?'

'Would he love you so well had you no fortune to recommend you?' I demanded. 'Knowing Wickham, I take leave to doubt it.'

Georgiana protested again but here the conversation was interrupted briefly by the arrival of our cousin Colonel Fitzwilliam.

'I came as soon as I received your message, sir,' he said to me, 'for I judged it a matter of some urgency. What is going forward here?'

'This silly chit imagines herself in love with Wickham,' I said.

'What?' Fitzwilliam burst into laughter and it was some time before he could be persuaded to take the matter seriously. This caused more annoyance to Georgiana than to myself.

'We have been careless in our guardianship, sir,' I told Fitzwilliam soberly. 'We should have enquired more closely into the character of Mrs Younge before we engaged her to be my sister's companion. It seems she had an acquaintance with Wickham and has done everything possible to further his interest with Georgiana. I doubt not he promised her some reward once his object was achieved. Heavens, what a dupe have I been. I make no doubt they have been planning this for some time.'

Fitzwilliam sucked in his breath. 'It is fortunate indeed that you happened upon them when you did.'

'The veriest chance,' I agreed. 'For it was mere impulse on my part to join Georgiana, here in Ramsgate. Had I been but a week later . . .'

'It is indeed quite frightening,' agreed Fitzwilliam. 'But you shall not take upon yourself more blame than your due, sir. Honest men cannot be expected to anticipate the actions of scoundrels.'

I could not be so easily reconciled. 'Wickham thinks he knows me,' I said intensely, 'but he does not. For had he succeeded in his design, he would not have lived to enjoy his ill-gotten gains. She would have been a widow as soon as she was a wife, for I would have killed him. Aye, and swung for it, if I had to.'

'You could not!' whispered Georgiana, appalled. 'You could not court death and dishonour in such a way!'

'Better tried and hanged for murder than the disgrace of knowing you were tied for life to such a man, and through my carelessness.'

'He means it,' cried Georgiana. 'Cousin, can you not talk some sense into him?'

'It has not happened, and it will not,' said Fitzwilliam with practical good sense. 'But it is well that you know how far your brother would go to protect you. You are the one we have to talk sense into, Georgie. You must understand what manner of man Wickham is.'

'I confess I do not,' said Georgiana. 'He always seems so gentle and good. And if he is everything you say, how was it that Papa esteemed him so highly? Could he really have been so blind?'

'He could and he was,' said Fitzwilliam bluntly. 'You know well enough that Wickham's father was a decent man: his good conduct as your father's steward naturally inclined your father to believe the son just as respectable. Wickham's manners were always charming, as we have lately been reminded. Your father was fond of him and enjoyed his company. He never understood Wickham's true nature.'

I took up the story. 'When he visited Pemberley, Wickham took care to guard his behaviour: Papa saw nothing to raise his suspicions. He was not so guarded at other times and in other places. We both saw enough to understand what he was, and we had reason to believe those things we heard about him, too. Georgiana, he is totally without principle.'

'I cannot believe he is so wholly lost,' said Georgiana tearfully. 'And he loves me, I know he does. I am sure he would change, for my sake.'

'I am sure he would not. If he really loved you, he would make some effort to re-establish a character and hope to win you when he had done so. He would not try to persuade a fifteen-year-old girl to an elopement, of that you may be sure.'

'He is all idleness and dissipation, Georgiana,' added Fitzwilliam. 'And you have a fortune which would enable him to live exactly as he chooses. I am sorry to give you pain, but you must face it, that is Wickham's design.'

'His chief design, certainly. I cannot help wondering if he has an additional motive. Had he succeeded, he would certainly feel he had revenged himself on me, would he not?'

'Revenged himself?' Georgiana turned to me. 'What have you done, sir, that he should wish to revenge himself?'

'Deprived him of the living at Kympton, or so he maintains,' I said. 'Papa hoped he would make the church his profession, as you know. That living was intended for Wickham as soon as it fell vacant. Long before it did, Wickham told me he had no intention of going into the church and asked if he might not reasonably expect some monetary compensation, instead. I agreed to that.'

Fitzwilliam was laughing again. 'Somehow, we were not quite happy with the notion of Wickham becoming a clergyman.'

'A devil's advocate, if ever there was one,' I agreed. 'Well, we paid him off. He had a bequest of a thousand pounds left to him in our father's Will and we gave him an additional three thousand on condition that he resigned all claims to the living, which he did. We have the documents which he signed at the time.'

'I confess, I have to admire his impudence,' said Fitzwilliam. 'He took the money and left debts all over Derbyshire, which your brother discharged as soon as it was known to us.'

Fitzwilliam often seemed to find some humour in Wickham's perfidy, which I myself have never perceived. 'I hoped I had seen the last of him,' I said. 'But three years later, when the living fell vacant, he informed me that he now had the intention of being ordained and felt sure I would present him with the living which Papa had intended for him.'

'Sir, how could he have done such a thing?' said Georgiana in astonishment.

'I still have his letter,' I assured her. 'He told me his circumstances were in a very bad way. He had professed to be studying the law, but that was a mere pretence. His substance had been squandered on his indulgences, mainly hazard, I believe. Never could he resist placing bets on a throw of the dice.'

'Is this true?' Georgiana turned to Fitzwilliam.

'Do you call your brother a liar?' Fitzwilliam was at once all severity.

'I ... er ... no! Sir, I beg your pardon. I am confused, that is all.'

'Well, it is not to be wondered at. You knew nothing of these matters and it is hardly surprising that you relied on your memory of Papa's good opinion. But even a father such as ours could be deceived, my dear.'

Georgiana sighed, knowing she must accept it. 'What do you mean to do now, sir?'

'Tomorrow I will take you to Rosings Park and place you under the care of our aunt, Lady Catherine. I am sorry you do not like the idea but, until I have found a new and proper companion for you, there is nothing else to be done. As for the rest, that is something I must discuss with Fitzwilliam. You may leave us, now.'

'You are tired and upset, Georgie,' said Fitzwilliam with more kindness, perhaps, than she deserved. 'Try to get some rest, and do not fret too much over Wickham. He is not worth your pain.'

But there were tears in her eyes as she went and we both knew there would be suffering for some time to come. 'Better this than what might have been,' observed Fitzwilliam.

Between us, we agreed that we could not let Georgiana's indiscretion become public knowledge. The affair must be kept as secret as possible, for the sake of her good name.

Unfortunately, the same consideration prevented any public exposure of Wickham. Since neither of us saw any value in confronting that gentleman, we merely despatched a letter, telling him that he would not be allowed to see my sister again and advising him to leave the place immediately.

I had heard nothing of him since and had supposed him to be in town for he is more inclined to city life than the countryside. Never had I expected to see him in Hertfordshire.

At first, I suspected him to be here because he had learnt of my own presence in the county and had some new scheme afoot, for always he seemed to look upon me as his own personal financier. In this, at least I did him an injustice, for when he saw me, he was clearly astonished, and looked as though he hardly knew how to support himself. But he recovered more quickly than I did and managed, damn his impudence, to touch his hat. I returned the salute and rode on, fuming with anger.

If Wickham was rusticating, I reflected, it must be because he had pressing reasons to get away from town. There could be no other explanation. But why he should have come to Meryton was beyond my comprehension.

Bingley joined me after taking his leave of the ladies and I said, 'You know most of the gossip, Bingley. Are there any young ladies of fortune hereabouts?'

Bingley would have his little joke. 'Heavens, Darcy! Never did I expect to hear that from you. What have you done? Lost all your fortune at faro?'

'Indeed, I have not!' I retorted. 'But I have just seen a known fortune hunter. Come, now, I am serious. I want to know what he is about.'

'Caroline is the only lady with any fortune that I know of, and I think she is safe enough. Who do you mean?'

'That gentleman with the Bennet sisters.'

'Do you mean Lieutenant Denny, the odd-looking cleric, or the tall, handsome one?'

'Was there an odd-looking cleric? I did not see him. No, I meant the other: George Wickham.'

'That name I have heard before,' said Bingley frowning. He looked at me. 'Did not you have some trouble with him once?'

'More than once,' I admitted. 'We need not concern ourselves with what is past. I am curious, however, to know what
brings him into Hertfordshire.'

'I gathered he has arrived but lately and is about to take up
a commission in the regiment.'

'Wickham? In the army?' I was all astonishment. I could
not imagine how he had raised enough money to purchase a
commission, or that he would use money for that purpose if he
had it.

Most likely he had found a benefactor, I thought. Always,
he was plausible and he could easily persuade someone to bestow favour upon him. On the other hand, someone less innocent might have felt it a small enough price to get rid of him.

Wickham's vanity would be gratified with the notion of
strutting around in a scarlet coat adored by all the ladies. He
would also, I was persuaded, believe regimental dress would
make him even more attractive to any passing heiress.

I had a more informed view of army life, gained from the
conversation of my cousin, Colonel Fitzwilliam, and it was one
I was sure Wickham had not considered. Regimental discipline, regimental training would be irksome indeed to a man
of his stamp.

Whoever had purchased Wickham's commission had my
fullest approval. Indeed, I wished I had thought of it myself.
Had I had the wit to think of it, I would have purchased for
him a commission in the regulars, for in the militia it was less
certain that he would be drafted into any military campaign.

I sighed for a lost opportunity: it would be diverting to entertain myself with pleasing notions of Wickham on the march and, best of all to my mind, Wickham on the battlefield!

I was recalled to the present when Bingley said, 'What do you wish me to do about the ball, Darcy? I had intended to send a general invitation to all the officers, but if this man is now among them, there could be some awkwardness.'

'There could indeed, should he be unwise enough to come,' I agreed. 'But I think he will not. Should he be foolish enough to do so, I shall know how to deal.'

'Darcy, I do not want trouble.'

'Would I cause any?' I smiled at him. 'You need not fear Wickham, my friend. What I would say to him would be short, to the point, and anyone hearing me would think no evil. But he would take my meaning, you may be sure of that.'

'Then I will follow my original intention and issue a general invitation to all the officers,' said Bingley, half-questioningly, waiting for my concurrence. 'Wickham, I will leave to your discretion.'

'He will not come.'

But my happy thoughts about Wickham in the army had vanished. For the winter, he would be quartered in Meryton and during that time his life would not be much troubled by regimental duties. I had heard Colonel Forster saying his officers were in need of rest and if that did not apply to a new recruit, Wickham would certainly enjoy the same benefits.

He would be here in Hertfordshire, where none had reason to suspect him and he would be received into society as warmly as all the other officers. Perhaps more so, for the insinuating charm that had enabled him to deceive Georgiana was always his greatest advantage.

Already, I had seen that charm at work upon Miss Elizabeth Bennet, and although it did not surprise me, I did not like it.

A few moments of reflection taught me Elizabeth could be in no danger from Wickham. I knew nothing of her fortune, but I could not suppose it to be large: and fortune was Wickham's chief design. That being so, he was unlikely to single out Elizabeth.

I shook off this concern and applied myself once again to the task of subduing my feelings for Miss Elizabeth Bennet.

It was by no means easy: whenever I reminded myself of her family and her low connections, an image of her face came into my mind, and she was laughing, as though she considered these objections quite absurd.

I knew they were not: I am Darcy, master of Pemberley. My family is ancient and, though untitled myself, I am of noble descent. Was I, then, to disgrace myself in the eyes of everyone by connecting myself to such an inferior family? I could not. I knew I could not. It was quite out of the question.

On Thursday, Bingley and his sisters sent out their invitations to the ball. They went personally to Longbourn to issue their invitation to the Bennet family. I declined the invitation to go with them. I had business letters to write and I made that my excuse.

When they returned, the ladies were full of giggles, which

they explained by telling me they had met an extremely odd relation of Mr Bennet.

They told me his name. They refused to tell me more. It was to be a surprise. They had included him in their invitation to the ball where I was to see him and judge him for myself without forming any preconceived ideas. They were eagerly anticipating whatever I might later have to say about him.

I looked at Bingley. He was laughing, too. 'Do your worst, Darcy, my lips are sealed. The girls have threatened me with death if I dare say a word.'

I frowned, for I had the feeling I had come across the name of Mr William Collins before, and not so very long ago, but I could not remember where. 'Well, at least you may tell me where he comes from?'

The three of them looked at each other and burst into fresh laughter. 'Oh, no! That is the best part of all. Oh, it is too rich! You would never believe how rich!'

The laughter continued until they had to wipe the tears from their eyes, and I perforce, could only watch them with growing unease.

Five

⋙

FOR THE NEXT FOUR DAYS THERE WAS SO MUCH RAIN that we were confined indoors for most of the time. I had no opportunity to learn anything about the mysterious Mr Collins.

This did not trouble me. Whatever had so diverted Bingley and his sisters would, no doubt, be explained in time. Though I confess I was dismayed to learn there were relations, even upon Mr Bennet's side of the family, who could occasion some ridicule.

I became angry with myself, for such dismay showed me I was wavering about what I should do, when I knew perfectly well what I must do. Although I had said nothing to my friends of my plan for departure, I intended, on Wednesday, to make some excuse to Bingley and take myself off to town, remaining there until I had conquered my feelings. Never again would I visit Netherfield until I was certain master of myself.

At present, I had not much thought to spare for Wednesday: my mind was occupied with Tuesday's ball, for I was going to dance with Elizabeth. Unwise it might be: the delight of doing so would, I knew, make the pain of leaving her harder to bear, but that I would face alone and in my own time.

On Monday, Bingley sought me out. 'This is a confounded nuisance, Darcy. A business matter has occurred and really, I ought to go into town today but I cannot, now the ball is arranged for tomorrow. But I must go on Wednesday, at the latest. Sorry I am to leave you with only the ladies and Mr Hurst for company, but it cannot be helped. I should be able to return on Saturday.'

'If I can be of any assistance,' I said, 'I would willingly go with you.' And remain in town when he returned.

'No, no, I thank you. It is merely a matter of drawing up some papers: stay here, Darcy, and keep the ladies company.'

I gave an inward sigh. The presence of Bingley's sisters and their demands upon my attention were not going to assist my endeavours to overcome my partiality for Elizabeth Bennet. For that I needed time alone, to reason myself out of it.

Tuesday dawned and as preparations for the ball began, we gentlemen escaped into the billiard room, leaving the ladies to give directions to the servants. At last, feeling strangely nervous, I went to dress for the ball.

The officers were the first to arrive and it did not surprise me Wickham was not among them. Afterwards came the Gouldings and the Lucases: several other families arrived before the Bennets made their appearance.

Elizabeth took my breath away: she wore the simplest of gowns in a deep rose-pink satin making all the more elaborate fashions there seem fussy and overstated. She was easily the most striking woman in the room: even her sister Jane paled into insignificance beside her.

I did not go near her until my heartbeat had settled into a more steady rhythm. When I did, I was quite taken aback by the short way she answered my greeting: however, she was equally short with Bingley and upon closer observation I perceived she was in some perturbation of mind.

I watched her move around the room, apparently looking for someone and felt absurdly gratified when I saw she had been seeking, not a gentleman, but rather her friend Charlotte Lucas. She drew that lady aside, and seemed to be spilling out her trouble.

Trusting her friend would succeed in restoring her usual good humour, I turned away, for I had other duties, other people to greet and be civil to. Eventually, I was able to stand back for a while.

A man's voice, spiced with malicious amusement, caught my attention. I looked up and saw Mr Bennet: he was treading backwards delicately, one arm around his eldest daughter. 'I will swear,' he said happily, 'I have not been so excessively diverted this last twelve months.'

The lady seemed equally diverted, although her voice held a hint of sympathy. 'Oh, poor Lizzy!'

I followed their gaze, seeking out 'poor Lizzy'. She was dancing prettily enough, but without, it seemed, much enjoyment. Then I caught sight of her partner, an awkward, thick-set fellow dressed in clerical garb, solemn-faced yet somehow quite ridiculous, moving wrong, scurrying back into position, moving wrong again, and causing stifled ripples of mirth among all who watched.

Poor Lizzy, indeed. Like Mr Bennet, I was more diverted than sympathetic. And why not? Miss Elizabeth Bennet had enjoyed more than one chuckle at my expense, it was a most unexpected pleasure to find that advantage was mine, if only for a moment.

It was clear she found nothing diverting in the situation. Had Miss Lucas succeeded in soothing her initial ill-humour traces of it had returned to her expression. I determined to wait a while before asking her to dance.

I partnered Caroline Bingley: Elizabeth was partnered by a scarlet coat and, I was relieved to see, more like herself by the end of the set. She returned to Miss Lucas and was in conversation with her when I approached to make a formal request for the honour of the next two dances.

There was something rather haughty but not unpleasing about her manner when she took her place opposite me. Her chin was tilted slightly, her mouth unsmiling, her eyes half hidden by her eyelids.

Something absurd and tender caught me by the throat: how I looked I know not, but I could not trust myself to speak and the dance commenced and continued for some time with no conversation between us.

'This particular dance fits well with the music,' observed Elizabeth, after a while.

'Yes, indeed,' I managed, astonished to discover my voice was perfectly sound.

The mouth curved, the eyelids lifted and the sparkle was there in her eyes. I waited with keen anticipation for whatever was coming next.

'Now it is your turn to say something, Mr Darcy. I talked about the dance and you should make some kind of remark about the size of the room or the number of couples.'

'I am your servant, madam. Whatever you bid me to say, that I will say.'

She nodded, rather like a governess teaching an awkward child. 'Very well, that reply will do for the present. Perhaps by and by, I may observe that private balls are much pleasanter than public ones: but now we may be silent.'

'Do you talk by rule while you are dancing?'

'Sometimes,' came the airy reply. 'One cannot be entirely silent for half an hour together. Yet for the advantage of some, conversation ought to be arranged so they may say as little as possible.'

By 'some', I suppose, she meant me. I asked whether she was consulting her own feelings or mine.

'Both,' she replied. She went on to say we were both of a taciturn disposition, unwilling to speak unless we said something amazing.

She was too intelligent to believe that about herself. I did not think it was true about me, either, though looking back on our acquaintance she might be excused for thinking so.

This conversation petered out and we danced for some time in silence. I found myself looking at her mouth, her lips slightly parted, slightly curved: I found myself wondering how it would feel to claim that mouth with my own, to—

I checked myself abruptly. To give my thoughts another direction I said the first thing that came into my head. 'Do you and your sisters often walk into Meryton?'

'Yes, quite often.' A pause and a sidelong look. 'When you met us there the other day, we had just been forming a new acquaintance.'

I stiffened. Damn it, I had forgotten Wickham. For the first time I realized how very odd that meeting must have appeared to Elizabeth: she had seen it, of course.

I did not wish to speak of Wickham but since I had, by my own thoughtlessness, led right into the subject, I felt I might take the opportunity to give her a warning. I said, 'Mr Wickham is blessed with such happy manners as may ensure his making friends. Whether he is equally capable of retaining them is less certain.'

'He has been so unlucky as to lose your friendship,' said Elizabeth, 'and in a manner which he is likely to suffer from all his life.'

I had no wish to go into that, especially now, when I was most eager to enjoy her company, and most painfully aware the precious minutes were passing by.

I did not have to, for our dance was interrupted by Sir William Lucas, who stopped us to pay his usual fulsome compliments. Such superior dancing was not often seen, my fair partner did me credit, and so on. He turned to Elizabeth and went on, 'I shall hope to have this pleasure often repeated, especially when a certain desirable event, my dear Miss Eliza, shall take place. What congratulations will then flow in!'

These words were accompanied by a significant look and I, following his glance, had it most forcibly brought home to me what he meant.

Bingley was dancing with Jane Bennet: Bingley had been paying Jane Bennet far more attention than was wise and, it seemed, he had given rise to a general expectation of their marriage at some time in the near future.

I stared at them, shocked to realize I had been too preoccupied with my own problems to pay much attention to what Bingley was about. And Bingley, far from considering the implications of what he was doing, was in a fair way to connecting himself with a family that could only be a continual cause of repugnance.

When Sir William left us, I pulled myself together and turned back to Elizabeth. 'Sir William's interruption has made me forget what we were talking of.'

'I do not think we were speaking at all. Sir William could not have interrupted any two people in the room who had less to say for themselves. We have tried two or three subjects already without success and what we are to speak of next I cannot imagine.'

I could not help smiling, and suggested we talk of books.

'Books? Oh, no! I cannot talk of books in a ballroom: my head is always full of something else.'

'The present always occupies you in such scenes, does it?'

'Yes, always,' said Elizabeth absently.

Whatever had crossed her mind had nothing to do with the present: I found myself being cross-examined about something I had said during her stay at Netherfield.

Now, she reminded me of the occasion. 'I remember hearing you once say, Mr Darcy, that you hardly ever forgave, that your resentment, once created, was unappeasable.'

She wanted to know how careful I was about my resentment being created. 'It is particularly incumbent on those who never change their opinions to be secure of judging properly at first.'

I asked why she was asking all these questions: she only smiled and said she was studying my character, without much success.

I confess, I was offended. It is not the kind of thing a young man likes to be told by the lady he loves. By now I was convinced that Wickham, in his insinuating way, had given Elizabeth some story to account for the coldness of the encounter she had witnessed.

It would not be a story to suggest he was at all to blame.

I had no intention of going into the subject. Instead, I suggested that she put off sketching my character for the present. 'There is reason to fear that the performance would reflect no credit on either.'

'If I do not take your likeness now, I may never have another opportunity.'

I made answer cold enough to show my displeasure and

neither of us spoke again. When the dance ended, we parted in silence, for I had no wish to subject her to the worst of my ill-humour.

I could not be angry with her for long, however, for I knew well enough who was really to blame. Wickham! My dance, my only dance with Elizabeth, spoilt by Wickham!

Well, that was it, and perhaps I should not repine too much. There had been moments I could remember with pleasure.

I danced next with Louisa Hurst, and afterwards spent a few minutes in conversation with the two sisters until Colonel Forster came to claim Miss Bingley for the next dance.

I took some wine and fell into a reverie, still unhappy about my dance with Elizabeth: then, to my astonishment and indignation, I found myself accosted by that same absurd cleric I had observed her dancing with earlier.

Someone should have taught him better manners. There had been no introduction and, had I wished for his acquaintance I would have sought it. But this fellow was beyond understanding his own impertinence.

Here was none other than the relation of the Bennets that Bingley and his sisters had found so ridiculous, Mr William Collins.

His intrusion was explained, if not excused. My aunt, Lady Catherine de Bourgh, had lately bestowed upon him the living of Hunsford, near to Rosings Park. He was, he said, delighted to be able to assure me that Lady Catherine and my cousin, Anne, were both quite well yesterday sennight.

This was just part of a long speech of equal inconsequence

and absurdity: I had not the patience to listen with proper attention. Instead, I found myself wondering what had possessed my aunt to grant him the living and, indeed, what on earth she found so pleasing in the oily fellow.

I could recall, now, how I had heard of him. My aunt is a diligent, I may even say a ruthless correspondent, and no detail is too trivial for her to pass on in her letters. Mr Collins had been mentioned. 'A most respectable young man,' she had told me, 'and so particularly attentive to me!'

I could easily believe it. Lady Catherine would favour him with invitations to Rosings, sometimes to dine, sometimes to spend an evening after dinner. She would expect him to make up a four at cards, to keep her informed of all that went on in the parish and to hear all her opinions and advice on every possible subject.

These attentions, it seemed, had given him an air of self-importance which I found intolerably offensive. When he came to the end of his speech, I said coldly, 'I am sure Lady Catherine could never bestow a favour unworthily.'

He would have launched into another speech had I not cut him short and walked away.

Another dance was due to begin but I did not trouble to find a partner: I had matters other than dancing on my mind, for I had not forgotten the information of Sir William Lucas. I was now resolved to observe for myself exactly what was between Bingley and Miss Jane Bennet.

I had seen at once that Bingley was in love with her. It came as no surprise, for I had known Bingley many years and he often fell in love.

This attachment, though, seemed stronger than anything I had previously witnessed. There was something earnest in his manner of conversing with her which suggested he had progressed beyond his usual light-hearted dalliance. He was taking her seriously and might indeed be contemplating matrimony. I knew he would not have given any consideration at all to the certain evils of such an alliance.

Had all the Bennets the agreeable manners of the two eldest girls, I would have had no hesitation in approving the match and wishing them well. The want of connection could not be so great an evil to my friend as it was to me: his family was respectable, and Bingley had received a gentleman's education, but he was not high born and his own fortune had, in his grandfather's day, been founded on trade. His sisters might give themselves airs and associate with people of rank but they themselves were not well connected.

But the other Bennets did not have the agreeable manners of the two eldest girls: Mr Bennet was intelligent, which made made him tolerable in spite of his sarcasm and indolence, but his wife had manners that were far from right and her lack of understanding made this impossible to remedy. Indeed, she encouraged the two youngest girls in their ignorance and folly, seeing no evil in the reputation they were acquiring.

I watched them, giggling, squealing and flirting outrageously with the officers and could not help feeling Mr Bennet should exert himself to do something about it. I had noticed Elizabeth making some attempt to check the behaviour of the younger girls but if the parents themselves did nothing sensible, there could be no hope of improvement.

The events of that evening confirmed me in all my worst opinions of the Bennet family. At supper, wanting to sit near to Elizabeth, I also found myself sitting near her mother. That lady was boasting in a loud voice to Lady Lucas of her own belief that Jane would soon be married to Bingley, finding it a matter for self-congratulation that Jane was a favourite with his sisters, that he lived only three miles from Longbourn, that he was such an agreeable man and so rich!

Indeed, the main circumstance was Bingley's wealth: Mrs Bennet mentioned Bingley's income with relish and fully expected this to benefit the rest of her family, besides giving her girls the opportunity of meeting other rich young men.

I listened in growing indignation and contempt. I saw Elizabeth speak in a low voice to her mother, and though I did not hear what she said, it was made clear enough by her mother's next words: 'And what is Mr Darcy to me, pray? I am sure we owe him no particular civility as to be obliged to say nothing he might not like to hear.'

For Elizabeth's sake I schooled my countenance into a steady expression and pretended not to hear, but I doubt she was deceived.

Mrs Bennet carried on, regardless of who might hear. Others caught her words and were no less disgusted than I was, but it seemed she had not the perception to observe this.

It was some time before she had exhausted the subject of Bingley and Jane. When she had, I heard a few allusions which I did not, at first, understand. Then, to my consternation, I became aware the lady also thought Elizabeth would soon be married. Consternation gave way to astonishment, for Mrs Bennet had no designs on me. The husband she intended for Elizabeth was none other than Mr William Collins.

Elizabeth wore her blank-faced expression, and now it was clear to me what had been the cause of all her ill-humour. Mr Collins had designs on Elizabeth and had been teasing her with attentions which were most unwelcome.

Mrs Bennet was going to be disappointed, for Elizabeth had no intention of gratifying her hopes. I smiled, confident enough to be diverted by the notion, for I now understood Elizabeth's eagerness to find Miss Lucas at the start of the evening. I thought it likely she had entreated that lady to spare her, if she could, from the man's attentions.

After supper, I set myself the task of discovering the extent of Jane Bennet's feelings for Bingley. I watched her closely, but I could detect no symptom of love. Her countenance was amiable, smiling, serene. She liked him; she enjoyed his attentions; she knew he liked her and I had no doubt she would marry him, if he asked her, for he had much to recommend him as a husband.

Had Bingley actually engaged the lady's feelings, then he would have to take the consequences, but I did not think he had. I had seen affection in her gaze, but only when she looked at Elizabeth.

Had she regarded Bingley with only half the affection she showed for her sister, I would have felt myself obliged to let matters take their course. I confess it came as a relief that she did not. I had no wish to wound her feelings but I had no compunction about ruining the hopes and expectations I supposed her to be entertaining.

I spent some time musing on the best way to detach Bingley from Jane Bennet and it seemed as if the rest of the Bennet family were determined to strengthen my resolution by exposing their own defects as much as possible.

Mary Bennet, always eager to display her accomplishments, seated herself at the pianoforte and obliged the company to sit through an interminable performance. Eventually, her father exerted himself to stop her, but with such sarcasm as to distress the girl and embarrass the rest of the company.

Mr Collins then drew the attention of everyone in the room. I had already discovered the fellow never made conversation: he made speeches. He made one now, beginning with the announcement that if he could sing he would be very happy to entertain us all, somehow digressing to his duties as a clergyman and his respect for his patroness (and other members of her family), concluding with a bow in my direction.

'Let us all give thanks that Mr Collins cannot sing,' sniggered Caroline Bingley. 'He would be certain to dedicate his song to you.'

'The parishioners of Hunsford have all my sympathy,' I said grimly. 'I shall have something to say to my aunt when next I write to her.'

Mrs Bennet approved of Mr Collins. She told Lady Lucas

he was a good, clever young man. Mr Bennet shook with silent laughter whilst Elizabeth compressed her lips in vexation.

There was but little relief when the dancing recommenced: the younger Bennets made an even worse exhibition of themselves than I had previously witnessed, chasing after the officers and shrieking with laughter.

Mr Collins stayed by Elizabeth, no doubt subjecting her to his absurd speeches for the rest of the evening. Charlotte Lucas joined them whenever she could.

At the end of the evening, the silly matchmaking designs of Mrs Bennet had the Longbourn party still waiting for their carriage a quarter of an hour after everyone else had gone.

When the carriage arrived, Elizabeth, the one I could least bear to part from, was the first to step inside.

We saw them off at last, but not before Mrs Bennet had pressed an invitation to dinner on Bingley. Bingley said he would be happy to accept as soon as he returned from London.

I remained silent: if I had my way—and I meant to—Bingley would not return from London. If I had my way—and I meant to—none of us would see the Bennets ever again.

Six

***

BINGLEY LEFT NETHERFIELD FOR LONDON EARLY
on the following day. I saw him off for, with so much on my
mind, I had slept but little.

'I am glad you are awake, Darcy,' he said, 'for I rather wanted a word with you.' He hesitated a moment. 'Last night . . .'

'Yes?' I asked, with sudden suspicion.

I was presented with a problem which was not the one up-
permost in my mind. He said: 'Jane was asking me all manner
of questions: it seems she and Elizabeth have heard some kind
of story from that man you detest so much, Wickham.'

'I suspected as much,' I said disdainfully.

'Well, they do not particularly want to believe it,' said Bingley, 'which shows they have good sense. But I did not wish to

disclose your business, Darcy, not without your permission. Although I vouched for your character, of course.'

'I thank you.'

'Jane says Lizzy is anxious to know the whole story,' he told me. 'And I think perhaps you should disclose it, Darcy, because if this man is slandering you, she is the one to trust. I know you do not like her very much but you may believe she is not as frivolous as she sometimes appears. Elizabeth Bennet commands a lot of respect in this neighbourhood. Oh, do not look at me like that. I know the idea of opening up your private affairs is repugnant to you: sometimes it is necessary to prevent a greater evil.'

'I will give the matter some thought,' I said, all astonishment to learn what strange ideas Bingley had regarding my opinion of Elizabeth.

Bingley gave me a friendly punch and urged me to do just that before stepping into his carriage and bidding me farewell.

I walked back to the house, deep in thought. I had been touched to learn the two ladies were disposed to believe in me, especially in the face of whatever falsehood Wickham had proposed. It was not the usual state of affairs, for Wickham's engaging manners could deceive even the most sceptical before his true nature was understood.

Perhaps I should have been more forthcoming with Elizabeth when I danced with her, for I knew she had been probing to get at the truth. Now, I was tempted to take Bingley's advice, seek her out and lay the whole truth before her, resolving her own doubts and giving a clear warning to the rest of the neighbourhood. It would also give me a chance to see her for one last time before I left Hertfordshire.

I shook my head, deciding against it. I was beginning to understand myself: I could be forever finding excuses to see her 'one last time'. This time I could not allow my resolve to weaken, for I had not only myself to consider, and my friend was in more danger even than I was. It was imperative, now, to extricate Bingley from what I could only regard as a most unhappy connection.

At breakfast, I discovered the events at the ball had also alerted the ladies to the danger Bingley was in. 'Really, it is all too tiresome,' complained Mrs Hurst. 'I do wish Charles would stop falling in love with every pretty face he sees. Jane Bennet is a sweet girl, but I am persuaded she is not quite right for my brother. What do you think, Mr Darcy?'

I told her what I thought, most emphatically.

Caroline Bingley looked most struck. 'I own I had not thought Charles to be quite as partial to her as that,' she admitted. 'But perhaps you are right. What do you suggest we do?'

'We must join your brother in London tomorrow at the latest,' I said. 'And we must persuade him to remain there.'

There was but one person of our party who objected to my plan, and greatly to my astonishment, Mr Hurst was of the opinion we should not interfere.

'Deuced fine woman,' he said of Jane Bennet. 'Bingley won't find another like her.'

'No one is disputing that,' I informed him coldly. 'Her family is the problem: you know my views on that subject.'

'If he does not object, why should you?'

'He has not given the matter proper consideration,' I said with finality.

Overruled by the rest of us, Mr Hurst said no more, but his objection had amazed me. I would not have expected him to have any opinion on the matter. He was a surly man who seemed to have no interest in anyone or anything apart from cards, sport, food and drink. His wife largely ignored him: we all did. I had once thought we seemed to carry him around with us like a piece of unwanted baggage.

For the rest of the day, we set about arranging the business of quitting Netherfield Park. Caroline Bingley wrote to Jane Bennet to inform her of our departure and the likelihood of none of us returning to Netherfield. It was necessary, but I confess I did not much care for the creamy smile on that lady's face as she wrote.

For myself, I took no pleasure in the matter. I bore no malice towards Jane Bennet and, certain as I was she would not be heartbroken, I knew she had entertained hopes of securing Bingley. She would be disappointed and possibly embarrassed by the swift and sudden defection of such a promising suitor.

I refused to think of Elizabeth; I refused to dwell on my own feelings. Instead, I set myself the task of marshalling my arguments to Bingley. I had no doubt of my own ability to persuade him: he had paid no heed to the evils of such a match, but I would describe them most emphatically. And I knew he would accept my assurance he had not won the lady's affection.

We set off for London the next day. Miss Bingley stayed with her sister in Grosvenor Street, where Mr Hurst had a house. I persuaded Bingley to quit his hotel and move into my house in Eaton Place.

Bingley had been very surprised to see us, and I lost no time in making known our reasons. It pained me to see how distressed he was, but I did not hesitate. 'I am sure she would marry you,' I said. 'She knows you would make a good husband and she knows it would be to her own advantage. She is amiable, I have no doubt she would make a pleasing wife. But . . .' I went on to list all the causes of repugnance: her low connections, the defects of her family, and my own absolute conviction that her affections were not engaged.

Bingley was clearly shaken. 'I never thought she cared as much for me as I do for her,' he admitted, 'But I did feel she had some regard for me.'

'I have seen no evidence of it,' I said. 'I have watched her most particularly. We know her sister Elizabeth has her affection, we have seen it, it is most pronounced. If there was half as much affection in her countenance when she looked at you I would not now be talking to you as I am.'

Bingley was silent for some time. At last he said, 'I will give the matter some thought.'

I did not press any further: I knew he would come to see the sense of what I had said.

I wished I could be more sympathetic, but the sense of what I had said was just as applicable to my own sentiments for Elizabeth and I was feeling pain on my own behalf as well as his.

Besides, I did not want sympathy: I just wanted peace to deal with my feelings in my own time and I thought Bingley also would prefer to be left alone.

One advantage of being in town again was that I was able to see Georgiana and discover for myself how she was. I had been rather concerned about her, for she was shy and awkward with strangers and never made friends easily. Even with myself she showed some reserve: the difference in our ages and my being invested with authority of a guardian inclined her to look upon me more as a father than a brother. Never had she shown so much spirit as she had in her defence of Wickham, which I had then had to crush. I felt all the perverseness of that situation.

Georgiana was surprised, though pleased, to see me and I engaged to take her to the theatre on Saturday. In the event, Bingley and his sisters joined us, the two ladies making such a fuss of her that I had but little chance to converse with her. But I observed her, saw she was looking well, and a quiet word with Mrs Annesley, her new companion, taught me she was no longer suffering from periods of dejection.

Many of our friends were already in town for the winter season: within a week, we had enough social engagements to keep us busy until the new year: Bingley did not mention returning to Netherfield. His decision was understood without being spoken.

One morning, about a fortnight after we had left Netherfield, Bingley and I were at breakfast when the post brought a letter from my aunt, Lady Catherine. My aunt's letters were usually full of the most trivial communications and I opened it and began reading without much interest, until my attention was horribly fixed by one piece of information concerning someone I knew.

Mr William Collins, my aunt had written, was going to be married to a lady in Hertfordshire. The wedding would take place at Longbourn.

'Good God, Darcy, whatever is the matter?' cried Bingley. 'You are as white as a sheet.'

'How can she do this?' I asked myself.

'What? Who? Darcy, whatever is wrong?'

I did not answer. I rose from the table and would have quitted the room except that Bingley, swift on his feet, intercepted me before I reached the door, repeating, 'Darcy, what is wrong?'

'For heaven's sake!' I shouted at him. 'Can you not see I wish to be left alone?' I pushed him out of my way and ran from the room.

I found sanctuary in the blue saloon: there I was almost doubled over with nausea. Elizabeth with the odious Mr Collins! It was insupportable! How could she? I had been as certain as possible she would have no truck with him. How could I have been so mistaken in her character?

Early as it was, I reached for the brandy, gasping as the raw spirit stung my throat. It helped to pull me from the worst of my imaginings, but other cold ideas were taking hold. To my dismay I found myself visualizing Elizabeth at Hunsford Parsonage: she would be neighbour to my aunt, called upon to

dine and take tea at Rosings Park, and assist to make up a qua-
drille table, and listen and defer to that lady's decided opinions
on every trivial matter.

Worse, I would have to see her. I would have to see her and
call her Mrs Collins! Every year, I spent Easter at Rosings;
every year, I would see a little more of her spirit disappear, for
disappear it would. If marriage to the voluble Mr Collins did
not entirely crush her, the additional weight of my aunt's force-
ful personality surely would do the rest.

I could not bear it. I thought of her future suffering and
raged against those who would cause it. I thought of her con-
senting to the marriage and raged against her for doing so. I
thought of her submitting to the disgusting embraces of the
slimy fellow and wanted to strangle them both. I paced up and
down the room, tearing my hair, half resolving to ride straight
down to Longbourn and put a stop to it.

Yet she must have chosen it herself. I knew her mother
wished the match and would pressure her to accept, but I
had never supposed Elizabeth to be wholly amenable to her
mother's wishes, and she would not shrink from that lady's displeasure. As for her father, I was persuaded he had no great
opinion of Mr Collins: indolent he might be, but he would support her in any refusal.

Her own choice then, and what right did I have to object?
I had renounced her myself, and in doing so I fully understood
she might one day take another man to be her husband. This
was the notion that gave me greatest pain, but I had not expected it to happen so soon, and I had comforted myself with the

reflection that I would know nothing of it. I had even prayed for blessings on her and for a man who could make her happy, but with Mr Collins there could be little prospect of that.

I reached for more brandy, changed my mind and slumped in a chair, disgusted with her, disgusted with myself for caring so much about a woman who had chosen such a fate, such a man!

How long I sat there, I know not. I heard Bingley go out: he must have spoken to the servants, for none disturbed me, not even to make up the fire. The ashes were cold in the grate long before I emerged from my reverie and even the sound of the doorbell, the sure signal of visitors, did not fully rouse me.

Had my visitor been any other than Georgiana, my butler would have said I was not at home, but he did not dare send away my sister with a false excuse. Instead, he showed her into a sitting-room at the back of the house, told her I was presently engaged in a matter of business, then came to inform me she was there.

I forced myself to some semblance of normality, tidied my hair, straightened my stock and slapped at my own cheeks to bring a little colour to them, for I did not wish my sister to be concerned about me.

She was with Mrs Annesley. I ordered tea, asked what she had been doing and obliged myself to make conversation. We discussed several matters before Georgiana asked, 'Did you meet a lady named Charlotte Lucas whilst you were in Hertfordshire, sir?'

I was surprised. 'Well, yes, I did. Why do you ask?'

'I wondered what she was like.'

'Not very tall, a little on the plump side, rather plain, I'm afraid. Straight brown hair; I cannot vouch for the colour of her eyes.'

'And what is your opinion of her?'

'My dear, I had but little conversation with her. She seemed a pleasant, calm, sensible sort of woman, but more than that I cannot tell you. Her father, I am afraid, is a dreadful bore. What is your interest in Miss Lucas?'

Georgiana shrugged. 'It is merely that I wondered what kind of woman would marry Mr Collins.'

I gasped, swallowed, and managed, 'What did you say?'

'Mr Collins,' said Georgiana, 'is the new rector of Hunsford, and our aunt, Lady Catherine—'

'Yes, yes, I know all that,' I told her. 'I have met him, for my sins.' I was trying to think, which in my dazed state of mind was not easy. To give myself time, I said, 'When did you meet him?'

Georgiana flushed. 'The last time I was at Rosings Park, of course. In July.'

'Ah, yes, of course. And where does Miss Lucas come into it?'

'Have you not heard from Aunt Catherine recently?'

'I have,' I confessed, 'but I have not—' I gasped as a new idea assailed me. 'I have not paid as much attention to her letter as perhaps I should have done. Mr Collins is to be married, you say?'

'To Miss Charlotte Lucas,' confirmed Georgiana. 'You find that astonishing?'

'It is astonishing,' I told Georgiana, 'because when I saw Mr Collins only two weeks ago, he was paying court to a very different lady. She did not welcome his attentions, but he was quite oblivious to the fact. He meant to pay his addresses to her, I am convinced. And once his purpose is fixed, I am persuaded nothing will shake it. But no.' I shook my head again. 'Even he could not propose to two women within a fortnight.'

Georgiana gave a little shriek of laughter. 'Less than a fortnight, for he returned to Hunsford last Saturday with the good news.'

'I wonder how she contrived it?' I said, supposing for a moment Elizabeth's sense of fun had led her to bring those two together. 'But no. She would not. I am persuaded she could not have wished Mr Collins for her friend.'

I turned my thoughts to what I had observed at the ball, recalling how Miss Lucas had joined Elizabeth often, with the kind intention, as I had thought, to give her friend some relief from Mr Collins. 'I wish I had paid more attention to what was going on in that quarter,' I said at last, 'but I confess I did not.'

'I am all bewilderment,' my sister complained. 'Tell a plain story, sir, I beg you.'

So I told as much as I was able, finding some relief in speaking of Elizabeth, describing her, if only briefly. Both my sister and her companion were diverted by my account of the dance she had endured with Mr Collins.

'I should like to meet Miss Bennet,' said Georgiana, surprising me. 'I remember thinking so when you mentioned her in your letter from Hertfordshire.'

I became aware of danger and switched to speaking of Miss Lucas. 'I am sure she will make an excellent wife for Mr Collins,' I said. 'I am delighted for him he could not have chosen better. Miss Lucas is a very sensible, practical lady.'

'But not as sensible as Miss Elizabeth Bennet,' observed Mrs Annesley shrewdly.

'Neither of them are fools,' I said indifferently, 'though their dispositions are not alike.'

I turned the conversation to another subject and when they left, I retrieved my own letter from Lady Catherine, reflecting that I could have saved myself a very unpleasant morning had I paid just a little more attention to the content.

But I could not wholly blame myself. Mr Collins had, at first, certainly chosen Elizabeth to be the future mistress of Hunsford Parsonage and the mention of Hertfordshire and Longbourn had done the rest, for I had no previous reason at all to suppose Miss Lucas had become involved.

I found it somewhat harder to satisfy myself on the point of my own violent objections to the notion of Elizabeth getting married. During the last fortnight, I felt I had made quite satisfactory progress in my attempts to subdue my own partiality for her.

At last, I persuaded myself I did not object to her marrying: should she find a man worthy of her regard, I would be the first to wish her joy. I simply felt Mr Collins would be an objectionable husband for her.

It was easier to excuse Miss Lucas for accepting a man for whom she could have no real regard. I suspected the lady had but little fortune and marriage was necessary to preserve her from future poverty. Mr Collins was respectable, and though she would find his company disagreeable, she would have some security and a comfortable establishment.

She would have a more comfortable establishment than I supposed, for on reading the rest of my aunt's letter I discovered the Longbourn estate was entailed away from the female line and, upon the death of Mr Bennet, Mr Collins would inherit.

My aunt did not approve of entails: for Mr Collins's sake she was glad of it but in general she saw no need for it. She went on to give me her very decided views on the matter. She ended by saying she hoped the present master of Longbourn had made decent provision for his daughters.

I hoped so too, but I had my doubts. In my own view, the five daughters were now explained as Mr Bennet's repeated attempts to father a son who would inherit the estate.

I now knew far more of Elizabeth's business than I had any right to know, and it pained me, for, like Miss Lucas, she and her sisters could scarcely avoid future poverty if they did not marry prudently.

I could not be sanguine about their prospects. With some fortune, they might at least be secure; with little or no fortune, such low connections, and the repugnance any man of sense must feel towards the family, even the undoubted charms of the two eldest girls were unlikely to save them from penury and want.

Mrs Bennet's determined pursuit of husbands for her

daughters could now be better understood: rapacious, she certainly was, but her motive of securing their future prosperity could not be despised.

Her methods could, but she was too silly to understand how obvious she was: she would never believe it was largely her own fault that her eldest daughter had been deprived of her best chance of future prosperity.

I had removed Bingley from the imprudent connection he was about to make; I had renounced Elizabeth and was determined to conquer whatever feelings I still had for her. The Bennets would have to make shift for themselves as best they could, for I could not repent my own decision. My duty was to myself, my family and my friends.

I hardened my heart against all the Bennets.

Seven

———

JUST BEFORE CHRISTMAS, GEORGIANA WAS TAKEN ill: it began as a trifling cold and quickly developed into an ague, with fever, aching limbs, headaches and a racking cough.

I cancelled all my engagements: in my anxiety, I frequented my sister's establishment more than my own, and it soon became clear that her companion, Mrs Annesley, had taken the same infection.

Our physician let some blood, prescribed some draughts and ordered both patients to stay in bed.

I instructed the housekeeper to attend to Mrs Annesley. I could, I suppose, have prevailed upon Bingley's sisters to watch over Georgiana but I did not: I found myself remembering how little real concern they had displayed when Jane

Bennet was ill. I found myself feeling most reluctant to place myself under any obligation to those two ladies.

It crossed my mind that my sister would have fared better had she had Elizabeth to look after her.

A gentleman undertaking the role of sick nurse would raise a few eyebrows in polite society, but I did not hesitate: I determined I myself would care for Georgiana.

Since nursing does not come within the scope of a gentleman's education, it was fortunate the housekeeper was a sensible woman, and after her initial astonishment and protests against my resolve, she gave sound, practical advice. 'Sir, you can only keep her warm, make her comfortable and give her medicine according to the doctor's instructions,' she said.

'Is that all?'

'Should she take a turn for the worse, we must summon the doctor again. But there is nothing you can do to bring about her recovery, which depends upon her own constitution. You can only make her comfortable.'

I took her advice and did everything in my power to make Georgiana comfortable. In addition, I ordered delicacies to tempt her appetite and read aloud to her when she wished it; only when she was sleeping did I venture out for air and exercise.

Thankfully, she began to mend and my enquiries after Mrs Annesley produced pleasing intelligence also.

Whilst she was ill, Georgiana had felt too wretched to care who attended her. Recovering, she displayed some embarrassment. 'Sir, you should not: it is not seemly.'

'Would you have preferred me to send for our aunt?'

'Indeed, I would not. But you, sir, have cancelled engagements and neglected your friends, and over Christmas, too!'

'Should any friend object to a little neglect in such a case, he is no longer my friend.'

'You are so good to me,' she said. 'I do not deserve it.'

'Oh, come now! Who else should look after you, with Mrs Annesley ill herself?'

'How is she?' asked Georgiana for the second time that evening.

'She is mending—you do like her, do you not?'

'Yes, I do. I never felt so much at ease with Mrs Younge, you know.'

'I did not know,' I said, startled. 'Why did you not speak to me of this?'

Georgiana looked away. 'I could not. I could find no reason for the way I felt and I was sure you would think me foolish.' She smiled faintly. 'Indeed, I thought myself foolish. Fitzwilliam says I should have trusted you better. He says foolish or not, you would have found a replacement had I made my wishes known.'

'Indeed I would. We may occasionally be obliged to tolerate people we do not like, my dear, but we do not have to employ them.'

'That is what Fitzwilliam said.' And then, answering my look of enquiry, she added, 'He came to see me when I was at Rosings Park. He talked a great deal, told me about things you would not tell.'

'The devil he did! I will have something to say to our cousin when next I see him.'

'You must not blame him for telling me. He said even when you were children, Wickham . . . Oh, I cannot speak his name without abhorrence! He said you were blamed and punished for things Wickham did. And that he laughed over it!' Georgiana was in tears and I hastened to comfort her.

'Silly little juggins,' I said fondly. 'It is past: it does not matter now. Fitzwilliam should not have distressed you.'

Perhaps my cousin was wiser than I thought, for Georgiana said, 'It cured me of any affection I felt for him: I hated him when I knew that! And, sir, I know how much it must have pained you when I . . . and I cannot tell you how sorry I am.'

'That is enough,' I said. 'We need not regard it. Come now, dry your eyes. Let me see that pretty smile of yours.'

She obliged me, but the smile soon faded and the serious look returned to her countenance. 'Fitzwilliam thinks Wickham is unstable,' she said. 'And, having been thwarted in his design, his resentment may lead him to impose on you in some other way. Sir, I beg you will have a care for yourself.'

'I do not fear Wickham,' I said. 'I never have. The worst he can do is elope with a sister of mine.'

This conversation and others which took place during her recovery marked a deepening of my affection for Georgiana. Always I had cared for her, but the difference in our ages had kept us apart. Now, we came to a new understanding and friendship. And in caring for my sister and learning of her, I became aware that the pain of parting from Elizabeth Bennet was at last beginning to subside.

The New Year had scarce begun before I discovered we were not wholly free of Bennets, after all. I had then returned to my own establishment. One day Miss Bingley called, demanding an immediate and private interview with me. I was annoyed, for I had been engaged in writing letters of business and I do not care to be interrupted at such times.

However, she brought intelligence of an alarming nature: Miss Jane Bennet had followed us to London.

'She is staying with her aunt and uncle in Cheapside,' said Miss Bingley, with distaste. 'And means to remain there for several months. I am convinced she entertains hopes of renewing her acquaintance with Charles, the scheming little hussy.'

'She has written to you, I take it?'

'Oh, yes. Very pretty sentiments, affecting to hope we shall be able to meet now and then. Such impertinence! As though our kindness towards her when she was ill at Netherfield gives her the right to impose herself on us whenever she wishes.'

It appeared the Cheapside relations had spent Christmas at Longbourn and had invited her to return with them to London.

I was of the opinion that Mrs Bennet had contrived the invitation, with the design of thrusting Jane at Bingley.

What Jane herself had in mind, I know not. I thought it would be astonishing had she come to town with no design of drawing Bingley back to her side. Though there was little to be gleaned from her letter, I felt she had understood our reasons for leaving Netherfield, and knew someone was her enemy.

'Well, at least she gave us warning,' I said. 'Which is foolish of her. It might be possible for her to meet your brother without ill consequence, but I doubt it. He has not, so far, expressed any admiration for any other lady, which, you must own, is unlike him.'

'So you think his regard for her is not yet sufficiently extinguished? So do I. We must endeavour to keep her away from Charles. I am persuaded it will be best if he does not know she is in town. We had better not mention it.'

I agreed, although reluctantly. I do not care for disguise of any sort but here we could not escape the necessity of it.

Miss Bingley said, 'She will call on us in Grosvenor Street, but we do not know when. Until that call has been paid, it would be unwise for Charles to visit us for he may chance upon her. Should he express any intention of calling, perhaps you could undertake to dissuade him.'

I nodded. Bingley would never have a great determination to go there and I could easily get him to put off any such intention.

'I suppose,' said Miss Bingley, 'Louisa and I will be obliged to return her call, but I shall not be encouraging. Has she hopes of meeting Charles through me, she will quickly learn her mistake. There is but little chance of her meeting him through any other mutual acquaintance: we move in very different circles from the Cheapside relations, I am sure.'

'Then there is nothing to cause concern.'

'There is the possibility of an accidental meeting.'

I shrugged. 'Should that happen, we will have to take the consequences. We cannot guard against chance.'

Miss Bingley looked dissatisfied with this answer, but I had no better one to offer. Bingley might meet his Jane in any public place, be it park, street, shop or theatre.

The consequence of such a meeting was most likely to be an unpleasant half-hour for me, for should Bingley discover Miss Bennet's presence in town I would not then deny my own knowledge of it. Bingley had the most amiable disposition, but even he would be angry to learn of this concealment.

I could not, however, feel any compunction: my motives were as they had always been, to save my friend from the certain evils, of an imprudent connection. I could not condemn myself for having done this much.

Jane Bennet called on the sisters ten days later. Miss Bingley told me she came at a moment when they were going out, and did not stay long. Meaning to be as discouraging as possible, they put off their return visit for two weeks. I confess, I did not blame them. Bingley himself might choose to protest, but the fact remains it does one no good, in our society, to admit acquaintance in that quarter of town.

Miss Bingley and her sister could be very chilly to anyone they wished to discourage: it did not surprise me when Miss Jane Bennet made no further overtures towards them. She remained in London, but six weeks went by without any word from her, and I began to feel easier. One might have supposed her motive for coming to town was simply to visit her relations.

The time was fast approaching when I was to leave London to visit my own relations. Always, I spent a fortnight over the Easter period with my aunt, Lady Catherine de Bourgh. As usual, Fitzwilliam would accompany me, but this year, hoping to strengthen the bond growing between us, I tried to persuade Georgiana to come, too. She was reluctant: always she was reluctant to visit Rosings, but this time I took some pains to get at the reason. In the end she confessed to feeling some distaste for our aunt and our cousin.

My sister's explanation was both reluctant and incoherent and it took some patience on my part to gain even a glimmer of understanding. At first, I thought it was about music.

Georgiana has a deep love and understanding of music and is extremely accomplished on both harp and pianoforte. She did not, she said, begrudge the hours of practise necessary to achieve the level of excellence she had attained. She was not conceited about her own performance: as yet, she had much to learn before she could be wholly satisfied with it.

Lady Catherine had never learnt: and my cousin Anne had been prevented from doing so by frequent ill health. Nevertheless, our aunt did not scruple to assert that no one had better taste or judgement in music than she and her daughter. Had they learnt, they would have been truly proficient, and with these self-awarded recommendations, Lady Catherine felt qualified to criticize Georgiana, abjure her to constant practice, suggest alterations to her performance and, absurdly, extol the superior musical gifts of our cousin.

Georgiana, recalling her early struggles to master her instruments, bitterly resented this. There had been times, she said, startling me, when she had practised till her fingers bled. She could not reproach our cousin for not learning, but she disliked the way Anne had, without exerting herself, smugly accepted the false value of her own superiority.

'I am sure Lady Catherine does not mean to be insulting,' I assured Georgiana. 'Indeed, often have I heard her speak of your talents with pride. You must not take it so personally.'

But I had mistaken her meaning, for Georgiana had spoken of music and my aunt's attitude simply as an illustration of her general character. And now she mentioned it, I had to concede there was a kind of pompous ignorance in my aunt, though never before had I known anyone be so severe on it as was my sister.

'Well, I will admit neither our aunt nor our cousin are the best of company,' I said. 'I will not press you to go, if you would rather not.'

She smiled her relief, and said, 'Fitzwilliam will be with you, will he not?'

'He will.'

'So you will not lack congenial company. I shall miss you, though. When do you go?'

'Next Monday week.'

'Then I shall see you again before you go.'

She did, only four days later and now she was saying she wished she had agreed to come, after all. 'But now I cannot, I have arranged to spend Easter with Chloe Bancroft and her parents. I cannot cry off. Such a pity.'

'How so?'

'Have you not heard from our aunt?'

'No, indeed. She would not write news she can impart when we arrive. Is there some new attraction at Rosings Park?'

'Lady Catherine writes Mrs Collins has visitors; her sister—er—Maria Lucas, is that right? A friend too, who I think must be that Hertfordshire lady I have heard you speak of. I confess I would like to meet her.'

I stared at Georgiana. 'Which Hertfordshire lady?'

'Miss Bennet.'

'Elizabeth Bennet?' I knew it must be. Mrs Collins was her particular friend.

So, I would see her again. The thought did not trouble me, for I had mastered my feelings. Although I still thought of her, it was with pleasure rather than pain and this discovery had taught me my heart was quite disengaged.

Now I was no longer tormented by my attraction for her, I was pleased by the prospect of seeing her again. Her company would be agreeable, especially at Rosings, and I would have the additional satisfaction of proving to myself, quite conclusively, that I had regained all the self-command I prized so much.

I was sorry Georgiana would not meet Elizabeth, for I was certain the two ladies would like each other very much. But on later reflection I saw it was, perhaps, better so: should my sister become friendly with Elizabeth, Bingley would hear of it and be reminded of Jane.

Although I could not be certain, I suspected Bingley had not gained mastery over his feelings for Jane as well as I had over Elizabeth. He was cheerful enough most of the time, but there were silences and I did occasionally spot signs of strain in his eyes. Most significant was that Bingley, even now, was not paying attention to any other lady.

Bingley's sisters were entertaining hopes of their brother taking an interest in Georgiana, but I quickly saw there was little likelihood of that occurring. They were polite and friendly each to the other but there was no spark to bring them together as a couple. For my own part, I was not sorry. Georgiana was but sixteen years old, and had too little worldly knowledge and too little self-assurance to be contemplating matrimony. As one of her guardians, it was in my power to give or withhold consent. I should not like to have been confronted by Bingley demanding my sister's hand in marriage.

Before I left for Rosings, I had told Bingley he was quite welcome to make use of my house in Eaton Place during my absence: he chose not to, preferring to join his sisters in Grosvenor Street. He went there on Palm Sunday, and on the following day I set out for Rosings with Fitzwilliam.

'So what have you been doing, sir, since last I saw you?' I asked my cousin as soon as we were settled down for the journey.

'Oh, the usual things. Lechery, debauchery and drunken ruts,' said Fitzwilliam with more humour than truth. 'And you?'

'Nothing so exciting,' I replied. 'Just falling in love and out again and rescuing a friend from the gorgon Medusa.'

Fitzwilliam was delighted. 'Tell me all.'

'About the gorgon? An absolute fright of a woman, I assure you. My friend was about to make her his mother-in-law. His lady-love herself hath charms a-plenty, but one cannot regard the family with anything but abhorrence. It was a close-run thing, though. Almost, I missed what he was about.'

'Almost, but not quite. I hope your friend is suitably grateful.'

'Not yet, but he will be.'

'I am sure he will. Now, I know you hoped I missed what you said about falling in love, but I did not. Come, sir, confess!'

'A hopeless passion,' I admitted, wishing I had kept a still tongue. 'But fortunately of short duration.'

'I find it astonishing,' said Fitzwilliam, 'that there exists a woman with charms enough to stir you for even a moment. I would know more of this lady. Her name, sir, if you please.'

'I shall not reveal it.'

'Ah! A married lady, I suppose?'

'You may suppose what you choose.'

'Well, you may be assured of my secrecy. I would not like to get you into trouble with Lady Catherine and our cousin.'

I grimaced. 'One day I shall be in trouble with Lady Catherine, you may be sure, unless our cousin finds herself a husband, and I despair of that happening.'

My own dear mother had been sister to Lady Catherine. I had been but four years old when my cousin Anne was born, and I have no doubt my mother agreed, at the time, it would be a fine thing were I to marry my cousin when we reached a suitable age. I do not accept it was a definite arrangement, so much as a pleasing notion. But ever since, my aunt has considered me engaged to her daughter. What was worse, despite warning hints from others in the family, Anne herself believed it.

I was sorry for my cousin, for Lady Catherine was doing her no service by such foolish persistence. My own father, when he had realized what she was about, had tactfully tried to reason with her and found there was nothing to be done about it. She was determined, and I said as much to Fitzwilliam.

'Then so must you be, should it come to a showdown,' said Fitzwilliam indifferently. He went on, 'Georgiana believed in the engagement, too, you know. I told her it was nonsense, but she might appreciate hearing it from you.'

'I did not know that. I will speak with her.'

We talked of Georgiana for a while and then I went on to tell Fitzwilliam the latest news of Wickham.

'In the army?' Fitzwilliam found that excessively diverting, as I had known he would. 'Why should England tremble?'

'I would not have believed it had I not seen it for myself. His regiment is in winter quarters in Hertfordshire at present, under the command of a man named Forster. Do you know him?'

'I have met him once or twice. He was engaged to a silly little piece about half his age. I suppose he is married to her, now.'

'You do not have a good opinion of him?'

'He is not strong on discipline, that is all I know of him. And with someone like Wickham amongst his officers, I think he needs to be.' Fitzwilliam brooded over the matter for a while, then added, 'They will be encamped at Brighton during the summer. Perhaps if I see Forster, I will drop him a hint. If it is not already too late.'

I had been wanting to prepare Fitzwilliam for Miss Elizabeth Bennet, but having been so unguarded as to tell him I had been in love, I had felt it wise to discuss other subjects before mentioning her, for I did not wish him to make any connection. As a prelude to mentioning Elizabeth, I asked my cousin if he had met Mr Collins.

Fitzwilliam looked surprised. 'I have. I confess, I am disappointed to learn you know of him. I was keeping him as a surprise for you.'

'Someone else did that, too.' I went on to describe how I had met him at the Netherfield ball. 'It seems I am to renew my acquaintance with several of the ladies I met in Hertfordshire, for Mrs Collins is one of them and she has her sister and a friend staying with her, at present.'

Fitzwilliam naturally quizzed me on the subject. I described all three, beginning with Mrs Collins and then going on to her sister. 'Maria Lucas is pretty in a china-doll sort of way,' I said, 'she is but fourteen or fifteen years old.'

'Pray, tell me,' said Fitzwilliam. 'I know you are saving the best until last.'

'Miss Elizabeth Bennet,' I said, 'is around twenty years old. She is dark haired, quite pretty, lively and clever. I am persuaded you will like her, but do not like her too much, Fitzwilliam. She has but little fortune.'

Fitzwilliam sighed, but I knew he had taken the hint. My

cousin could not afford to marry without paying some attention to money. As a younger son, he had but a modest fortune
himself and had been brought up to habits of expense which
made him dependent. His wife, if he took one, would need a
fortune to match his own at the very least.

'Does she play? Does she sing?' asked Fitzwilliam.

'She does,' I affirmed. 'Very prettily.'

'Then at least she will be a welcome relief at Rosings,' he said.

I said no more about Elizabeth and our conversation turned
to matters within Fitzwilliam's own family, for his brother, the
viscount, and his wife were expecting an interesting event and
hoped their firstborn would be a son. 'They're talking of nam-
ing him Fitzwilliam,' said my cousin in disgust. 'Imagine it,
Darcy! Fitzwilliam Fitzwilliam!'

I made a suitable answer and our conversation continued
until we reached Rosings Park. As we turned into the gates,
we spotted Mr Collins waiting to make his bow as our carriage
passed. Fitzwilliam wondered if he had been there all morning.

'Certain it is,' I said, 'the ladies at the parsonage will learn
of our arrival even before my aunt.'

Our first evening at Rosings was spent listening to my aunt's
authoritative voice speaking on the affairs of everyone in the
district and giving her opinions on all of them. In due course,
she embarked on the subject of those at the parsonage.

My aunt described Mr Collins as a 'very good, clever young
man'. I stared at her, all astonishment, recalling I had heard
Mrs Bennet also express that opinion. From that lady it was
not so surprising, but I had thought my aunt more discerning.

My aunt held the opinion that Mrs Collins was a quiet, sensible lady: she had, somehow, also become acquainted with her father, Sir William Lucas. 'One of nature's gentlemen,' my aunt pronounced, 'although I believe he kept a shop before his elevation to the knighthood.'

Maria Lucas was a pretty child who did not have much to say for herself. Miss Elizabeth Bennet was a very pretty, genteel sort of girl, my aunt supposed, 'But upon my word, she expresses her opinions very decidedly for one so young.'

Fitzwilliam raised an eyebrow at me, a look I returned with a half smile. And later, when we were alone together, he said, 'Do you suppose Miss Bennet actually dared to disagree with Lady Catherine?'

'I would not find it astonishing,' I admitted. I confess I found some pleasure in speaking of Elizabeth, now I was no longer tormented by an attachment for her. I went on, 'Miss Bennet has a lively sense of humour and would, no doubt, find it diverting to trifle with my aunt's curiosity.'

'I am impatient to become acquainted with this lively lady.'

'I expect we will see her at church, if not before.'

Mr Collins came to Rosings the next morning to pay his respects. Fitzwilliam greeted him good-humouredly: I bowed and remembered to congratulate him upon his marriage. 'I look forward to renewing my acquaintance with Mrs Collins,' I told him, which gratified him enormously and produced one of his long, pompous speeches of no consequence whatever.

Fitzwilliam flickered an eyelid at me, and suggested we should both repair to the parsonage immediately to pay our respects to the ladies within. Mr Collins was quite overcome by such a striking civility.

As we set off to walk the half-mile distance to the parsonage, I could easily account for my own excitement. I anticipated great pleasure and satisfaction in seeing Miss Elizabeth Bennet and knowing I was no longer in her power.

We arrived at the parsonage; we were shown into the presence of the ladies; and, at the very first sight of Elizabeth, my insides turned upside down.

To my utter mortification, I discovered the whole desperate struggle was about to begin again, for I was just as much in love with her as ever.

Eight

THERE WAS ONLY ONE THING TO BE DONE ABOUT IT. I determined I must stay away from her as much as possible. Several times during the next few days I excused myself to my relations and went out alone, to walk and rage and struggle with myself.

I know not how I had so far deceived myself as to believe my feelings for her had vanished, but the vexation of my spirits on discovering my mistake was the only circumstance which had given me a tolerable appearance of composure during our visit to the parsonage.

Elizabeth had scarce looked at me. A flicker of a glance when she curtsied, and the usual civilities had been all she admitted: I confess I had little enough to say, myself.

Fitzwilliam had immediately entered into conversation with

all the ladies: it was clear they were taken with him and perhaps this was fortunate, for my silence went unnoticed.

I had managed, after a while, to so far gain command of myself to ask after the health of Elizabeth's family. She assured me they were all well, then disconcerted me completely by informing me her sister Jane had been in London for the last three months. 'Have you never happened to see her there?'

I swallowed, and forced myself to say I had not had that pleasure. I was perfectly sure she was already sensible of the fact. I hardly knew how to look. It put an end to my efforts of making conversation.

When we left, Fitzwilliam reproached me for not having told him the half of it. 'Quite pretty!' he repeated my own words scornfully. 'Heavens, man, she is beautiful! And never have I met a lady with such happy manners! Easter at Rosings Park,' he added, 'might just be tolerable after all.'

Fitzwilliam called at the parsonage several times during the following week. I avoided the temptation to accompany him, instead taking myself off, either on foot or horseback.

I soon discovered even this occupation to be fraught with danger, for I had forgotten my information that Elizabeth, too, was in the habit of roaming the countryside. Once, I almost ran across her: only by great good fortune did I see her in time to strike into another path without being observed.

When we attended service on Good Friday, it took all the solemnity of that awful day to keep my mind on religious observance and not on the slight figure who stood on the north side of the church.

On Easter Sunday, after church, my aunt invited Mr Collins and his company to come to Rosings in the evening. I had time to brace myself and when they joined us in the drawing-room, I was able to meet Elizabeth with tolerable composure.

Fitzwilliam left me to listen to my aunt's conversation, making it clear he was going to monopolize Elizabeth. For a time I was content, thankful even, for him to do so. He seated himself beside her: it soon became clear he had found many subjects of conversation to interest her and I found my attention was continually straying towards them.

A surge of bitterness consumed me as I watched them together. I wanted to join in: I was too far away to hear their discussion, but it was clearly far more interesting than my aunt's conversation.

After a while, my aunt noticed she was no longer the centre of attention: she called out to Fitzwilliam, demanding to know what they were talking about.

They were talking about music, Fitzwilliam told her. To my acute embarrassment and true to my sister's word, my aunt then claimed to be the foremost authority on the subject, the only superior to my cousin Anne. Having established this, she asked, 'How does Georgiana get on, Darcy?'

'Extremely well, madam. I venture to protest there are few of her age who have such a thorough working knowledge of their instruments as my sister. Or, indeed, such a feeling for musical expression.'

My aunt instructed me to tell her to practise more. I thought of bleeding fingers and said coldly, 'She does not need such advice, madam. She practises very constantly.'

My aunt, having silenced the conversation between Fitzwilliam and Elizabeth, went on to patronize that lady. 'I have told Miss Bennet that she will never play really well unless she practises more. She cannot expect to excel if she does not practise a great deal.'

After coffee, Fitzwilliam persuaded Elizabeth to play for him and drew up a chair next to her at the pianoforte. To my intense annoyance, my aunt insisted on talking to me, interrupting my own enjoyment of Elizabeth's performance.

At last, I could take no more. My aunt could keep her dreary conversation until I had nothing better to listen to. My cousin Fitzwilliam, I decided, had had Elizabeth to himself for long enough. I left my seat and strolled over to stand beside the pianoforte, finding a spot where I had a perfect view of Elizabeth.

She immediately bestowed upon me her most mischievous smile. 'You mean to frighten me, Mr Darcy, by coming in all this state to hear me. But I will not be alarmed, even though your sister does play so well.'

I knew she did not really suspect me of entertaining any such design, and I said so. 'I have had the pleasure of your acquaintance long enough to know that you occasionally find great enjoyment in expressing opinions which, in fact, are not your own.'

She laughed, and turned to Fitzwilliam. 'Your cousin will give you a very pretty notion of me and teach you not to believe a word I say. I am unlucky in meeting a person so well able to expose my real character in a part of the world where I hoped to pass myself off with credit.' Then she turned back to me, and told me I was provoking her to retaliate. '. . . and such things may come out as will shock your relations to hear.'

The silent laughter in her eyes made my insides melt. I smiled and told her I was not afraid of her.

Perhaps I should have been, for when Fitzwilliam asked her what she had to accuse me of, she recollected the first time she had seen me, at the Meryton assembly. 'And what do you think he did?'

I, who was remembering perfectly well what I did, felt the heat underneath my collar.

'He danced only four dances!' She shook her head sadly at Fitzwilliam. 'I am sorry to pain you, but so it was. Only four dances, though gentlemen were scarce and more than one young lady was sitting down without a partner. Mr Darcy, you cannot deny it.'

She was generous enough to make no mention of the worst of it, but I knew she was thinking of it. Yet there was laughter in her eyes as she looked at me and perhaps a little kindness, too. Nevertheless, I felt the reproof and could only mutter a lame excuse about not knowing any lady beyond my own party.

'And nobody can ever be introduced in a ballroom!' She made the nonsense sound like the worst kind of impropriety. My cousin laughed and tut-tutted, enjoying my embarrassment.

Elizabeth asked what we would like her to play next, indicating she would let the subject drop, but now I could not help myself. I tried again, admitting I would have done better to seek an introduction. 'But I am ill-qualified to recommend myself to strangers.'

'Shall we ask your cousin the reason?' said Elizabeth, still addressing Fitzwilliam. 'Shall we ask why a man of sense and education, who has been about in the world, is ill-qualified to recommend himself to strangers?'

Fitzwilliam told her I would not take the trouble.

'Some people,' I said with a cold glance at Fitzwilliam, 'possess the talent of conversing easily with those they have never seen before. I confess, I do not. I cannot catch their tone of conversation as I often see done.'

Elizabeth was playing something soft and soothing. She talked as she played. 'My fingers do not move over this instrument in the masterly way achieved by so many women. But then, I have always believed it to be my own fault—because I would not take the trouble of practising.'

I thought of Georgiana and bleeding fingers and of her awkward, crippling shyness with strangers, comparing her with Elizabeth, who played well enough to please without torturing herself and had enough self-confidence to be satisfied with that. I thought perhaps Elizabeth had the better philosophy.

I told Elizabeth she was perfectly right: she had employed her time much better. She stared at me, her hands stopping their music in surprise. 'No one admitted to the privilege of hearing you can think anything wanting,' I went on. 'We neither of us perform to strangers.'

My aunt chose that moment to interrupt, putting an end to all possibility of pursuing the conversation. Elizabeth immediately began playing again. My aunt insisted on telling me Miss Bennet would play much better if she practised more, though, of course, her performance would never equal what my cousin Anne would have achieved had her health allowed her to learn.

I saw the faintest hint of amusement curve Elizabeth's mouth and wished my aunt would stop her absurdities. She did not, however: she continued her criticisms of Elizabeth's performance and added many instructions on execution and taste. How Elizabeth remained civil and forbearing, I know not.

I found myself wishing Fitzwilliam would take my aunt away and engage her in conversation at the other side of the room, leaving me to enjoy Elizabeth's company in peace. I quickly saw he was wishing I would perform that service for him. Our eyes met, like two cats trying to stare each other out: neither of us would give way.

After each piece, Fitzwilliam and I persuaded Elizabeth to play again and, at last, my aunt moved away to voice her opinions into the more receptive ears of Mr Collins.

Having observed all my struggles against Elizabeth had, so far, had the contrariest effect, that night, when I retired to my bedchamber, I abandoned struggle, allowed myself to think of her and gave free rein to my feelings, perhaps reasoning that once I acknowledged them, I would deal with them more easily.

It was a mistake. The force of my passion gripped me in spasm after spasm: I could barely keep myself from groaning aloud.

At last, sleepless and bemused, I rose and paced my bedchamber, shocked and desperate and bewildered to discover such feelings could have been awakened against my will, without my own knowledge or consent.

I had no power to conquer these feelings: I knew it and acknowledged it and, in so doing, I understood it remained only to determine what was to be done. My choices were clear, for with feelings such as these I could never offer myself to any other woman. I had to accept it: either I must remain single, loving her secretly, or I must give serious consideration to the idea of marrying her.

I winced as I thought of her family; I winced as I thought of her low connections: in taking her, I knew I would attract the ridicule and contempt of all my relations and friends and I felt all the disgrace of such an alliance.

But already I was scheming as to how her connections could be managed.

I had always intended, upon marrying, to live at Pemberley. And Pemberley, in the northern part of Derbyshire, was roughly 150 miles from Hertfordshire, a considerable and happy distance from her family. I would certainly allow Elizabeth frequent visits from her favourite sister, Jane, for that lady was pleasing enough. Mr Bennet, too, had an intelligence which made him tolerable and I could bear his company.

I did not think Elizabeth would press me to accept the rest. Although there would be times when I must admit the society of her mother and younger sisters, there were ways of making sure those times were of short duration. Should Elizabeth wish to visit Longbourn, I would permit it, but I would not accompany her. Should I discover in her any degree of affection for her Cheapside relations she could visit them when we were in town, but I would not encourage that, and never would I admit their society myself.

This was the best that could be done, and perhaps life would indeed be tolerable without the worst of her relations. In the dark, in the night, it all seemed quite acceptable. In the morning I was more alive to what it would cost me. The connections would be there, whether I accepted them or not: that was the worst aspect of the whole case.

After breakfast I took myself off for another walk, determined to empty my mind for a while. A break from thought, a break from feeling, fresh air, exercise, and perhaps then I would be able to think more clearly.

I had arrived at the parsonage. How it happened I know not, for I certainly made no conscious decision to visit, but I found myself pressing the doorbell. On being admitted, I was astonished to find Elizabeth, and only Elizabeth, in the room. I stammered an apology for intruding on her, saying I had understood all the ladies to be within.

She told me Mrs Collins and her sister had gone into the village, invited me to sit down, asked after Rosings and then, after a few moments of silence, she made enquiries after the

Bingleys and asked me what my friend intended to do with Netherfield.

She might have been making conversation, or she might have the design of discovering what had happened to make her sister's suitor quit the place so suddenly: she could not, however, have chosen a subject more injurious to her own prospects of securing me, for I was then reminded, most forcibly, of all the follies and indiscretions of her closest relations at the Netherfield ball.

She persisted with her questions. 'I think I have understood that Mr Bingley has not much idea of ever returning to Netherfield again? It would be better for the neighbourhood that he should give up the place entirely, for then we might possibly get a settled family there. But perhaps Mr Bingley did not take the house so much for the convenience of the neighbourhood as for his own, and we must expect him to keep it or quit it on the same principle.'

I told her coolly that Bingley would probably give up Netherfield if a suitable purchase offered.

Elizabeth did not answer. Neither did she introduce any other subject of conversation: the silence lengthened and then it seemed to me as though I was hearing again those teasing words she had spoken as we danced together.

'Now it's your turn to say something, Mr Darcy. . . .'

Someone had to say something.

'You ought to make some kind of remark on the size of the room. . . .'

I made some remark on the way the parsonage had been

made comfortable and, in the hope of showing her my aunt had her good points, I added, 'Lady Catherine, I believe, did a great deal to it when Mr Collins first came to Hunsford.'

'I believe she did—and I am sure she could not have bestowed her kindness on a more grateful object.'

Knowing Elizabeth, I could not be quite sure how this was meant. I went on, 'Mr Collins appears very fortunate in his choice of a wife.'

'Yes, indeed; my friend is one of the very few sensible women who would have accepted him and made him happy—though I am not certain I consider her marrying Mr Collins the wisest thing she ever did. She seems perfectly happy, however, and in a prudential light, it is certainly a very good match for her.'

Casting about me for something else to say, I remarked it must be agreeable for Mrs Collins to be settled within such an easy distance from her own family and friends.

'An easy distance?' Elizabeth stared at me. 'It is nearly fifty miles! I should never have said Mrs Collins was settled near her family.'

I could not help smiling. 'It is proof of your own attachment to Hertfordshire. Anything beyond the very neighbourhood of Longbourn, I suppose, would appear far.'

Her colour rose: perhaps she thought I had been patronizing, for she said sharply: 'Where there is fortune to make the expense of travelling unimportant, distance is no evil. But that is not the case here. Mr and Mrs Collins have a comfortable income, but not such a one as will allow frequent journeys—and

I am persuaded my friend would not call herself near her family in under half the present distance.'

This was a new point of view for me, but not one I wanted to consider at the moment. I had fortune enough to make the cost of travel negligible, but Pemberley was a long way from Hertfordshire and I was concerned: I knew not the exact degree of affection she felt for her family, but I had to suppose she cared for them more than I did and might feel the distance and separation more keenly than I would wish.

I said persuasively, 'You cannot have a right to such a very strong local attachment. You cannot have been always at Longbourn.'

Elizabeth looked at me in astonishment and I realized the direction the conversation had taken. I drew back in some confusion: it seemed my reflections during the night had taken hold of me and I was beginning to pursue my interest with her before I had properly made up my mind.

It was time to change the subject: I asked if she was pleased with Kent. She answered, and we had a stilted conversation on that subject until Mrs Collins returned to the house with her sister.

They looked surprised to see me. I said I had intruded on Miss Bennet by mistake, supposing they were all at home.

Mrs Collins glanced at Elizabeth, then at me again: something in her look told me she had suspicions. I left as soon as I could.

When I wrote next to Georgiana, I told her enough about Elizabeth to incline her favourably towards the lady. I said nothing about my own inclinations, though it occurred to me that should my sister be willing to accept Elizabeth, I might not care too much for other opinions.

During the next week, I called at the parsonage every day, sometimes alone, more often with Fitzwilliam and once my aunt accompanied us. I found it difficult to talk, especially as I now knew myself to be the object of scrutiny from Mrs Collins. When that lady heard my cousin Fitzwilliam laughing at me for being so tongue-tied, her interest deepened, making everything worse. I knew she had the advantage of remembering some of the incidents which had occurred in Hertfordshire and I was persuaded she understood me.

Time was passing and I was still no closer to making up my mind. We were to leave Rosings on Saturday, but when my aunt pressed us to stay longer, I agreed to remain another week. Had my aunt understood my motive she would have been most indignant, but she did not, and chose to take it as a compliment to herself and my cousin Anne.

Elizabeth's habit of wandering the countryside now became a matter of interest to me. There was a grove on one side of the park with a pleasant sheltered path; once, I had seen her there and avoided her, but now, desiring her company away from the constraints placed upon me by the presence of others, I wanted to know if she often frequented that spot. I went there myself, waited awhile and found myself rewarded: she came, and was so far encouraging as to inform me it was her favourite haunt.

I met her there several times, after that. I asked how she

liked being at Hunsford and about her love of solitary walks and was fairly soon satisfied: her attachment to Hertfordshire was not so great as to cause her any deep pain to leave it, or any desire for frequent visits. I was persuaded she would prefer the wilder beauties of Derbyshire, which would more than adequately compensate for whatever favourite places she had to leave.

She liked the countryside in Kent, too. Our visits to Rosings would be no hardship for her, especially as she had a friend living in the parsonage. I supposed I might have to tolerate the society of the unctuous Mr Collins rather more than I did at present, but if I gritted my teeth, I could bear it for half an hour, now and again.

My own feeling about that gentleman made me wonder how any sensible person could tolerate his society and, curious on the subject, I asked Elizabeth for her opinions on the happiness of Mr and Mrs Collins.

'They seem to be tolerably happy together,' she replied. 'My friend has an excellent understanding and manages her own and her husband's domestic felicity with remarkable insight.'

She would say no more, but there was a glimmer in her eyes and I saw she found the subject diverting. She had some understanding I was not privy to, nor was I likely to be, since it would have been most improper for her to entertain me on the subject of her friend's marriage.

Such reservations increased my desire for the kind of confidence between us that could exist only in marriage. I began to comprehend she was exactly the kind of woman who would most suit me. The way she had nursed her sister proved she could be caring and affectionate. She would, as my aunt put it, 'express her opinions very decidedly' which made a refreshing change from those who constantly deferred to mine. But most of all, it was the ease and liveliness of her disposition which appealed to me and which would, I knew, temper my own, more serious nature.

Yet still, the thought of connecting myself with such a decidedly inferior family was anathema to me. The consequences of doing so could be distressing indeed. I recalled one of Miss Bingley's taunts on the subject: *Do let the portraits of your uncle and aunt Philips be placed in the gallery at Pemberley. Put them next to your great uncle, the judge. They are in the same profession you know: only in different lines.'*

I winced and resolved I would not go to the grove again.

I went to the grove again, in spite of my resolve. This time, to my absolute rage, she was not alone: Fitzwilliam was with her, all attention, chatting away, making her laugh. I could see that any interruption to their tête-à-tête would be very unwelcome indeed.

They did not see me. I turned and walked away, furious and bitter as I reflected on what I had seen. Clearly Fitzwilliam wanted her for himself: he was exerting himself to engage her affections and she was by no means averse to his attentions.

I could not bear it. The thought of losing her to my own cousin was too painful to contemplate. I raged against myself for agreeing to stay at Rosings another week: had we left when planned, this could not have happened. I was persuaded he was, at that very moment, proposing to her.

I wondered how I was going to stop it. I despaired, knowing I could not stop it. My imagination leapt forward: I saw them coming up to Rosings, announcing their good news; I saw myself obliged to congratulate the pair of them; I saw myself as groomsman at their wedding; I saw myself obliged to propose a toast to the happy couple.

In the end I calmed down and tried to think in a more rational manner. Fitzwilliam, I told myself, knew very well he could not afford to marry a lady with no fortune. He had no intentions. He had simply come across Elizabeth on one of her walks and, naturally, he was escorting her back to the parsonage. I tried to reassure myself there was no more to it, but I could not help suspecting them.

He returned alone to Rosings. I watched him, but could detect no particular excitement in his manner, he seemed much as usual. He looked pleased when my aunt informed us she had invited Mr Collins and company to drink tea at Rosings that evening, but only said he hoped Miss Bennet would not think it too much of an imposition if we prevailed upon her once more to entertain us with some music.

Still I suspected him: I was resolved to watch them together that evening, and determine for myself, if I could, the extent of their involvement with each other.

To my utter confusion, the others arrived that evening without Elizabeth. Mr Collins was most profuse in his apologies to my aunt. 'My cousin sends her humble apologies and most earnestly begs you will forgive and excuse her for not accepting your ladyship's most kindly bestowed invitation. She is, indeed, most unwell, and I am persuaded nothing but the most severe headache could prevail upon her to absent herself from the very great kindness and condescension of your ladyship's company.'

I was all astonishment. Elizabeth? With a headache? It was possible, I supposed, but it did not sound at all like her. I glanced at Mrs Collins and saw she was watching me, a little smile playing at the corners of her mouth.

Fitzwilliam expressed his disappointment and concern and begged Mrs Collins would, upon her return, convey his best wishes to Miss Bennet for a speedy recovery. Lady Catherine conceded, rather grudgingly, that if Miss Bennet were unwell, then, of course, she must be excused. When I could find my voice, I said I hoped she would soon be better.

That look from Mrs Collins had my mind in turmoil: I was persuaded she knew of my feelings and had alerted Elizabeth. I recalled a slight embarrassment in Elizabeth when I had seen her last, and saw this must account for it. She must have been wishing me to declare myself.

I thought she must have been disappointed, today, when she met Fitzwilliam instead of myself: I thought she might have stayed away purposely, this evening, to give me a clear opportunity of finding her alone at the parsonage.

I drank tea and debated with myself whether to go: I knew that even if I did not, Mrs Collins would report my disturbance to her friend. I recalled the pain when I had so foolishly thought I might lose her to Fitzwilliam.

And later I found myself ringing the doorbell at the parsonage.

Nine

❧

I THREW DOWN MY PEN, SHUFFLED THE SHEETS into order and began to read through my own letter, wincing here and there at the things I had been obliged to write.

For a moment I was tempted to tear it up: it was not the kind of letter I should like to receive and Elizabeth would not like me any better for reading what I had to say. I knew, however, that nothing could give her a worse opinion of me than the one she now held.

Last night, still smarting from having seen her with Fitzwilliam, confused by the quizzical look from Mrs Collins, desirous of solitude in which to reflect, I had excused myself from the party at Rosings.

Repulsed, still, by the idea of connecting myself with her relations, I had, nevertheless, found myself walking to the parsonage. I persuaded myself I was concerned about her health: I persuaded myself I was simply visiting.

I had not been there five minutes before I was blurting out how ardently I admired and loved her.

Now I wished I had not. It had been the worst, the most bitterly humiliating experience of my life.

All my regard, all my struggles, counted for nothing with her. She cared not at all that I was prepared to disgrace myself for love of her, that I was prepared to face the derision of the world by making her my wife.

So far from being flattered by my declaration, she had rejected me with an incivility which bordered on contempt.

'... I have never desired your good opinion and you have certainly bestowed it most unwillingly. ...'

Worse was to follow:

'... do you think that any consideration would tempt me to accept the hand of a man who has been the means of ruining the happiness of a most beloved sister?'

Shaken and dismayed, knowing my own cause was lost, I had found a mean satisfaction in admitting my part in separating my friend from her sister. I told her I rejoiced in my success. 'Towards him I have been kinder than towards myself.'

She ignored this, for she had another accusation to fling at me: to my utmost incredulity, I now learnt that she held me responsible for wantonly and cruelly blighting the life of George Wickham.

I will not repeat what she had to say on the subject: evident it was that Wickham had imposed on her with some falsehood: evident also that she believed it.

I had been too angry to defend myself. Now, though still bitter, I was capable of cool rational thought. I saw that, however my pride revolted against imposing on her yet again, my own reputation required me to give an explanation.

In my letter, I told her of my reasons for separating Bingley from her sister. It pained me to do so, for I knew what I said about the defects of her closest relations must cause her distress; the necessity, however, could not be helped.

I went on to assert my own belief that Jane Bennet's affections had not been engaged, but even as I did so I began to feel distinctly uneasy. Elizabeth said I had 'ruined her happiness' and I had to admit she was likely to have better information than myself. I went to some trouble to emphasize that, if I had inflicted pain on her sister, it was unknowingly done, as a result of my own impartial observation.

I described the means by which I had detached Bingley from her sister, making no secret of his regard for her, allowing that only my own conviction of her indifference had persuaded him not to return to Hertfordshire. My connivance in concealing Jane's presence in town was admitted also, though I could not deny I felt some pangs of conscience there.

Dealing with Elizabeth's misapprehensions about George Wickham took longer. I had no idea what form of falsehood he had used against me, although I suspected it would be some kind of half-truth, for that was Wickham's usual way: I thought it most likely I had been accused of going against my father's wishes and depriving him of the living intended for him.

I will not repeat everything I wrote to Elizabeth. It is enough to say that I described Wickham's character, his connection with my family and my dealings with him in the matter of my father's Will.

It cost me no little pain to reveal my sister's intended elopement and for a while I hesitated, wondering if it was necessary. Only when it occurred to me Elizabeth herself might be in some danger from Wickham did I perceive that, for her own sake, I must reveal the whole of his character. So, assuring Elizabeth I had no doubt of her secrecy, and excusing Georgiana as best I could, I made that disclosure.

It remained only to add that my cousin, Colonel Fitzwilliam knew every particular of these matters and would, should she wish to consult him, vouch for the truth of my assertions.

I took my letter and went out to the grove, waiting there for some time in the hope of meeting her.

At last, she came. She turned away when she saw me, but I called her name and she turned back, reluctantly. Her face was pale and her eyes unfriendly but she took my letter. I bowed and felt my throat tighten as I took my final look at her.

She would not open my letter with any expectation of pleasure, but she would open it and she would read it.

Knowing it would keep her occupied for some time, I returned to the parsonage, this time to take my leave of those within. Mrs Collins pressed me to sit down and wait. 'Lizzy is out walking again: I am sure she will be sorry to miss you.'

My better information told me she would not be sorry at all, but I was thankful to infer that Elizabeth had not confided in her friend. I said I had seen Miss Bennet and had spoken to her. In no mood to listen to Mr Collins, I took my leave as soon as I could.

Back at Rosings, Fitzwilliam was at breakfast. I could not eat, but I took some tea whilst I considered how much to tell him. I could not bring myself to confide the whole of it.

In the end, I merely said it had come to my attention that Miss Bennet was on friendly terms with Wickham and, knowing what he was, I had felt obliged to inform her of his true nature.

'If she is partial to him,' I said, keeping tight control of my own composure, 'and I suspect she is, then she may be unwilling to accept my assertions. I have recommended you as my witness in these matters and I would be obliged, Fitzwilliam, if you would give her the opportunity to consult you today, should she wish to do so.'

'Yes, of course,' said Fitzwilliam, looking startled. 'How much may I tell her? You surely would not wish her to know . . . ?'

'I have told her everything,' I admitted. 'I set it down in a letter, so she might refer to it whenever she wishes.'

'Georgiana?' Fitzwilliam sucked in his breath as I nodded confirmation. 'You have taken a risk there, Darcy.'

'I think not.'

'I hope you are right. I had no idea she knew Wickham, or I would have warned her myself. How is she acquainted with him?'

'I told you: his regiment is stationed in Meryton, barely a mile from her home.'

'Oh, yes, of course. I had not previously made that connection.'

He gazed into his teacup as though seeking inspiration, then added, 'She may be friendly with him, but I do not think she can be at all partial towards him. She has been at Hunsford now for five or six weeks and will remain for another week at least. I cannot feel she would agree to such a long separation were she harbouring any tender feelings towards him.'

I seized upon that line of reasoning with some relief. 'I hope you are right.'

By the time Fitzwilliam set off for the parsonage, an hour had elapsed since I had put my letter into her hand. She had had sufficient time to read it and draw her conclusions. She would know how far she wished to question my cousin.

Unable to support the idea of remaining in the company of my aunt and cousin, I had my horse saddled and took myself off, wishful of putting as much distance between myself and Hunsford as I could.

I confess I galloped recklessly that day, and it would have served me right if some accident had befallen me. None did, however, and at last, rather shamed by the way I had used the beast, I dismounted and let him graze whilst I, taking advantage of the lonely spot, seated myself on a convenient tree stump and struggled to come to terms with Elizabeth's contemptuous rejection of my suit.

'. . . I have never desired your good opinion, and you have certainly bestowed it most unwillingly.'

I felt a surge of the most bitter resentment: I had told her I loved her enough to overlook her low connections and I had gone so far as to pay her the greatest compliment a man could pay a woman: and that was to be my answer.

'... why, with so evident a design of offending and insulting me, you chose to tell me you liked me against your will, against your reason and even against your character?'

All this, because I had been honest and told her of my struggles and the scruples which had so long prevented me from forming any serious design on her.

'You could not have made me the offer of your hand in any possible way that would have tempted me to accept it.'

My cousin Anne is a lady of consequence and heiress to the estate of Rosings Park, yet I could have married her any time this last six years. I could keep her waiting another six years and still she would have me. Caroline Bingley is a lady of some fortune, if not so well connected: she would continue to plague me with her attentions, never giving up hope of flattering me into her coils.

There had been, and still were, other ladies who deferred to my opinions, offered every attention, and thought and spoke and looked for my approbation. And always there were new-comers into society, ladies who very quickly took an interest in Fitzwilliam Darcy when they learnt he was master of great estates and had a vast fortune.

My father had told me I would be sought after. I had not given it much thought until he mentioned it, but when he did, I knew it was true.

That conversation between us took place when we both knew he was dying and his purpose had been to inform me of Lady Catherine's scheme of marrying me to my cousin Anne. After we had exchanged our views on the subject, he added, 'You will be master of Pemberley before the year is out. You understand your future, do you not?'

'I do, sir.'

'You are young for the responsibility, but you are equal to it, I think. However, there are pitfalls and you must be on your guard. You will find your aunt is not the only mama who schemes to marry you to her daughter.'

'That I have discovered already, sir.'

'You have given no lady cause to reproach you, I hope?'

'I have not.'

'That is well. It is easy, all too easy, for a young man who is courted and flattered to believe himself in love. Take care: be certain your lady is a proper match for you, for you will be married a long time. An unfortunate marriage could be the ruin of you.'

'I am not so easily beguiled, sir.'

But I had, perhaps, been beguiled by so many attentions into the belief that I could have any woman I wanted. I had never suffered a moment's doubt about securing Elizabeth.

'. . . *your arrogance, your conceit* . . .'

In justice to myself I have to say I was not conceited enough to imagine Elizabeth returned my feelings with the same fervour I felt for her. But I had, I confess, been persuaded she liked me well enough. And I had thought the material advantages of marriage to me would have been enough to secure any woman in her circumstances.

With her father's estate entailed on Mr Collins, her hopes of future prosperity were bleak indeed. I could not feel she had fortune enough to give her a decent income: only marriage could preserve her from want. Marriage to me would have done more than that: it would have given her riches, it would have given her consequence in the world and it would have secured the financial comfort of her family.

'. . . *do you think any consideration would tempt me. . . ?*'

Yes, of course, I did. I am a man of the world, I know how matters are arranged. I knew her situation. With her want of fortune, her vulgar connections, she must know she had little hope of making a good marriage. To secure the affection of a man like myself, an affection strong enough to overcome every rational objection would, for a woman in her circumstances, be considered a triumph indeed.

'. . . *I had not known you a month before I felt you were the last man in the world I could ever be prevailed on to marry.*'

I flinched, knowing that even in the bitterness of my resentment I was moved to a new admiration and respect.

What a mockery she had made of all my rational objections! I could have spared myself the whole struggle. Her low connections, the folly and imprudence of her mother and younger sisters were not to be any concern of mine. Elizabeth herself had put forward the one objection which could cancel all the others: she wanted none of me.

She had spared me from the embarrassment of such connections. Perhaps I should be glad of it? But I could not: wiser now than I had been yesterday, I knew I would rather have her good opinion than any other.

'You could not have made me the offer of your hand in any possible way that would have tempted me to accept it.'

All my thoughts twisted and taunted and jeered as I recalled that other, that most humiliating of indictments:

'. . . had you behaved in a more gentleman-like manner.'

With all her words bell-beating in my brain, I could no longer remain seated. I got up, paced around, kicked savagely at a clump of nettles, pushed my hands deep into my pockets and stared morosely into the misty green woodlands.

'I have every reason in the world to think ill of you.'

I had never given any thought to the possibility that Wickham might prejudice her against me. Looking back, I could hardly believe my own folly in not anticipating the mischief he might cause. If my own knowledge of him was not enough to warn me, and it should have been, I had also received definite information on the subject from Bingley.

I could easily comprehend now: I had been too ready to believe Bingley's assertion that I had the good opinion of the two eldest Bennet sisters. I had no doubt Bingley himself believed it: Jane Bennet would pursue her enquiries in a delicate manner, giving no hint of disapprobation.

I recalled Elizabeth's more robust attempts to probe into the matter when we had been dancing together at Netherfield. I had been angry, but I could not accuse her of giving me no opportunity to enlighten her: she had sought the truth and received no answer.

After this came our hasty departure from Netherfield. Until last night, I had given no thought to Elizabeth's view of the matter, never even considered she might resent it. Clearly, she had perceived my design had been to detach Bingley from her sister: add this to her dislike of me and her belief in Wickham was assured. She might have suspected, even, that Wickham's presence in Hertfordshire gave me yet another motive for leaving.

My letter, endorsed by the assertions of Fitzwilliam, might overthrow her good opinion of Wickham: it could do little to improve her opinion of me. She would acquit me of cruelty towards him, she might regret having done me an injustice, but she would easily comprehend my own attitudes and behaviour had done much to encourage her misapprehensions.

And there was another cause for disapprobation, one which more nearly concerned her, that of separating Bingley from her sister.

'. . . *the unjust and ungenerous part you acted* there *involving them both in misery of the acutest kind.*'

Had I really misled myself into inflicting pain on Jane Bennet? I did not know the lady well enough to judge. I could assert that in her appearance she showed no sign of special regard for Bingley, but I had given no thought to her character. Should her disposition lead her to conceal her feelings, then I might indeed have fallen into grave error.

Now, with hindsight, it took no stretch of imagination to comprehend Jane Bennet as a modest lady who would not wish to display her affection for a gentleman in the presence of inquisitive and impertinent neighbours.

Elizabeth, most likely in her sister's confidence, could hardly be mistaken in her belief of Jane's affection. And I knew Bingley still cherished tender feelings for Jane. He did not speak of them: he did not need to. His silences, the hint of strain in his eyes, and the fact that no other lady had taken his fancy during the last four months was enough to convince me this attachment was of a more enduring kind than any I had previously witnessed in him.

'Can you deny that you have done it?'

I could not: I had separated them without feeling the least compunction. If I could plead ignorance of Jane Bennet's true feelings, I could not deny awareness of Bingley's attachment.

I had separated them for reasons which seemed compelling, at the time. Now, in the light of my own pursuit of Elizabeth, my interference in Bingley's affairs seemed absurdly presumptuous.

Always an adept at finding excuses for myself, I found I was dismissing the affair between Bingley and Jane as unimportant, an affection that had been the growth of only a few weeks.

I caught myself doing it, and stopped myself, appalled at my own hypocrisy. I had no right to judge the affair on those grounds, for my own attachment to Elizabeth had grown just as quickly.

I had given no thought to my friend when I had blundered into the parsonage, last night. Having determined that Bingley should forsake his Jane, I had then gone about the business of trying to secure her sister for myself. Even when Elizabeth confronted me with the realization, I had felt no remorse, not even embarrassment. All I had felt, at the time, was a certain impatience, as though their affections, their miseries, were nothing in comparison with my own.

'... *your selfish disdain for the feelings of others* ...'

Her reproofs were beginning to strike home.

'... *your arrogance, your conceit* ...'

Every review of my own past behaviour was becoming a source of vexation and regret. I recalled my petulant disdain when I refused to dance with her at the Meryton assembly and even I could not excuse myself for that. With a deepening sense of shame, I recalled my resolve to ignore her on that last day when she had been staying at Netherfield. Occupied with my own disapproval of her family, I was determined to crush any expectations I might have raised. Never once had I considered she might disapprove of me.

I had ignored the mischief that was likely to occur wherever Wickham went, and I had compounded this folly by separating Bingley from her sister.

If I was kind to myself, I would still have to say my manner of proposing to her was ill-judged: if I was honest, I could only regard it as the worst kind of insolence.

For, I am ashamed to say, I had been far more eloquent on the subject of pride than I had of love, explaining how the consequence of my family would be wounded by connection with her own inferior relations and how my own better judgement was opposed to such an inclination, but such rational objections had been unable to overcome the strength of my attachment.

Miss Bennet had disdained the strength of my attachment.

'The feelings which, you tell me, have long prevented the acknowledgment of your regard, can have little difficulty in overcoming it, after this . . .'

There was no consolation in reflecting that, had I been more circumspect in the way I had paid my addresses, I would not have been more fortunate.

'. . . I had not known you a month before I felt you were the last man in the world whom I could ever be prevailed on to marry.'

She had detested me right from the very beginning.

'. . . the mode of your declaration . . . spared me the concern which I might have felt in refusing you, had you behaved in a more gentleman-like manner.'

'. . . had you behaved in a more gentleman-like manner.'

'. . . had you behaved . . .'

Her words sounded repeatedly in my brain and I actually put my hands over my ears as though I could blot out the tormenting reproofs. But I could not. Neither could I deny their justice.

It had been all my own doing: I would never see her again.

I had lost her.

I knew not how I was going to support myself.

Ten

—∞∞∞—

Time had passed and I had to pull myself together: I must return to Rosings and, much as I craved solitude, I knew I would have to endure the company of my relations throughout the evening.

A freshening wind whipped some colour into my cheeks as I rode back at a steady canter and I presented myself at dinner with an appearance of normality. I toyed with my food and no one appeared to notice how little I ate.

When the ladies withdrew, Fitzwilliam and I were left alone in the dining-room. He filled my glass and his own, and said, 'Miss Bennet was out walking when I arrived at the parsonage, this morning. I waited over an hour, but she did not return. So I have been unable to fulfil your commission, sir. Do you wish me to make another attempt? I could go down to the parsonage again, this evening.'

I stared at Fitzwilliam, my thoughts busy, calculating the length of time she had been out: over two hours! I could not believe my letter had held her attention all that time.

'I am sorry, Fitzwilliam, what did you say?'

'I see no reason to add my word to yours; Miss Bennet must know you would not make up a story about your own sister.'

'Perhaps you are right.'

'Of course I am. What is wrong with you, Darcy? You are not usually so dull-witted.'

'I beg your pardon. I am rather tired this evening.' I drank some wine and made an effort to rouse myself.

'I think I may have done enough, at all events,' he told me. 'I spoke to Mrs Collins: such a sensible woman. One wonders how she can bear to be married to such a numbskull. Well, I told her I had heard Miss Bennet was acquainted with Wickham and suggested she should drop a word of warning in her friend's ear because I knew of several occasions when his conduct had not been quite right. I did not go into particulars, but I daresay Miss Bennet will recognize greater import, should her friend pass the message on.'

'Yes. Thank you, Fitzwilliam.'

'We need have no fear of any partiality for him blinding her to the truth. Miss Lucas tells me Wickham has been courting an heiress since Christmas: and Mrs Collins says Elizabeth is quite untroubled by it. She is certain about that, and ladies have great penetration in these matters, you know.'

I could not deny the lady had penetration in my own case, but I had doubts of her fully understanding her friend: she, who had married Mr Collins to preserve herself from want, would scarce comprehend the higher principles which governed Elizabeth.

I only said, 'So Wickham has another heiress in his sights, does he? Let us hope the lady has a diligent guardian.'

When we joined the ladies in the drawing-room, my aunt perceived I was out of spirits, but immediately attributed that to the fact of our leaving tomorrow. 'But really, there is no need for you to go. Why do you not delay your departure for another week? If you did that,' she added, 'you could take Miss Lucas and Miss Bennet as far as London in your own carriage, and spare them the obligation of travelling post.'

I could think of nothing Miss Bennet would dislike more, but I only said, 'I regret, madam, I must be in London tomorrow.'

'Oh, well, if you must, you must. But I cannot bear the idea of two young ladies travelling post, by themselves! It is most improper.'

'I expect Mrs Collins will send a servant with them.'

My aunt said she would put it to Mrs Collins. 'Or perhaps I might persuade the young ladies to stay another month, when I can take them into town in my own carriage. You would not object to their company, would you, Anne?'

'I would not object, Mama, but I thought the ladies were to join Miss Bennet's sister in town, next week.'

My aunt immediately decided Miss Jane Bennet could stay in town another month, regardless of the wishes or convenience of the lady, or her relations. I swallowed and wished my aunt would stop talking about the Bennet sisters.

It was the greatest relief, at last, to find myself in the solitude of my own bedchamber. With a mind so occupied, it had been difficult indeed to listen to my aunt's conversation and I think I took care to answer her with civility only because Elizabeth's reproofs were so fresh in my mind.

'... *had you behaved in a more gentleman-like manner.*'

How those words tortured me. Every review of my own past behaviour brought home their justice and my sense of shame was severe indeed.

I had not expected to sleep at all: but I had not slept last night, either, and when a drowsiness began to overtake me, I gave in to it gratefully, thankful to be granted a few hours of oblivion before I had to face the world again.

I slept as though I had been drugged.

I awoke feeling sluggish and stupid. The business of dressing took twice as long as usual and my valet regarded me in some concern and asked if I were ill.

I was ready at last, went downstairs to breakfast, ate a little, talked a little, eventually took leave of my relations and settled into my carriage with Fitzwilliam.

By this time I had shaken off the sluggish aftermath of sleep, and now I knew I felt decidedly odd, but in a way that was not illness. It was neither pleasant nor unpleasant, and I could not quite understand it. I felt like a stranger to myself.

Mr Collins was at the lodge gates, waiting to make a bow to us as we passed. I shook my head, thinking he was not such a bad fellow, for all his parading and absurdity. He was respectable, happy in his situation and as sincere as a man with his limitations could be. Next time we met, I resolved to be more patient with him.

It was some time before it struck me as strange I should now feel so kindly towards Mr Collins, a man I had barely been able to tolerate only two days ago.

'. . . *your selfish disdain* . . .'

Elizabeth's reproofs were having an effect.

Elizabeth would be in town next weekend. I swallowed, wishing I could see her. She planned to spend a few days at her aunt's home in Cheapside before returning to Hertfordshire with Jane.

Jane Bennet was still in town! I started at the realization, knowing I must grasp the opportunity to make confession to Bingley, giving him time to see her before she left.

Bingley would be angry, and rightly so, to learn of my interference in his affairs, but I could not hesitate. I had felt myself justified when I believed Jane Bennet indifferent: now that I had better information, it would be wickedness indeed to conceal her presence in town.

As soon as he knew, Bingley, I was persuaded, would visit Jane Bennet in Gracechurch Street. I felt he would have little difficulty in assuring her he had previously been ignorant of her visit to town and, once that was accomplished, matters would take their course.

We arrived in London by one o'clock. After a cold luncheon, Fitzwilliam then transferred to his father's carriage, which had been sent for him, for he was to travel on into Derbyshire. I returned, thankfully, to the solitude of my own house in Eaton Place.

There, I discovered all my fine plans for Bingley's felicity had been overset even before they were made. A letter from that gentleman awaited me.

Caroline Bingley had once complained of her brother's letters. 'Charles writes in the most careless way imaginable,' she said. 'He leaves out half his words, and blots the rest.'

This letter was no exception. I spent half an hour studying one page and understood only that for some illegible reason, Bingley had gone somewhere, with someone, for a length of time which was specified but unreadable.

It might yet be possible to recover him in time to send him to his Jane and with the object of discovering where he was, I went to call in Grosvenor Street. The house was shut up. Presuming Mr Hurst and the sisters were Bingley's companions, I then called at Georgiana's establishment, hoping she would be able to give me more information.

She could not. She had stayed at the Bancrofts until Tuesday and had heard nothing of Bingley or his sisters. She spoke for some time of her own visit and enquired about mine.

'How did you get on with the lovely Miss Bennet?' she asked shyly.

I recalled, with some consternation, how I had mentioned Elizabeth in glowing terms in my last letter to Georgiana. Judging by the expression on her countenance, I had excited some expectations. How I managed to reply with composure, I know not. I said the lady was as lovely as ever and Fitzwilliam was very taken with her.

Georgiana looked disappointed. In thinking how well the two ladies would have liked each other, and how my sister could not fail to have benefited from knowing Elizabeth, I was struck with fresh pangs of grief and loss.

It would not do: I pulled myself together and made conversation as best I could. I left after half an hour.

Unless Bingley soon returned, I could do nothing about his affairs. I set aside his problem, determined to face my own.

During the next few weeks, I strove to appear as usual whenever I found myself in company and I believe I succeeded well enough, for no one remarked any difference in me. But the despondency of my spirits was great indeed. I found solitude was my greatest relief, and I sought it whenever I could.

My reflections were most unhappy: Elizabeth's reproofs had forced me to take a critical look at myself and I did not like what I saw. I began to comprehend how shallow and unworthy were my objections to her family: I loved her, but even in love I had been selfish, putting my own consequence before any other consideration.

Her accusations of arrogance, conceit and selfishness began to receive assistance in the most painful way, for unbidden memories of my childhood and youth now intruded. Events that had troubled me not at all at the time of their occurrence now presented themselves to me in a very different light, as evidence of these failings.

I cannot describe my horror in discovering how very selfish

and overbearing I had been all my life. All I can say for myself is that I had never before realised it. I could not now conceive why my parents had done so little to correct me, for they had been good themselves. My mother, to be sure, had some of that dignity which characterized my aunt, but without the absurdity. My father had been always most benevolent and amiable.

They had given me good principles; they had taught me good manners. I could wish they had taught me to correct my temper, but I had only myself to blame for the pride and conceit which had so recently been my undoing.

Often, during that time, I would experience those strange feelings which I had first noticed in myself on the day I left Rosings. Some change was taking place in me, partly through my own reflections, but mainly, I suspect, because of her reproofs. Wishful of change, I did not try to stop it. The lessons I was learning were painful, but the pain was deserved.

Still more painful was the prospect before me now. My future looked bleak indeed, for whatever resolutions I made, enlightenment had come too late to spare me the wretchedness of losing Elizabeth. How I wished I had learnt my lessons before I met her, instead of after I had lost her.

Bingley returned to town three weeks after myself. He looked surprised when I asked where he had been. 'Did you not receive my letter?'

'I received,' I said, 'a piece of paper filled with illegible handwriting and blots. I would not dignify it by calling it a letter. Bingley, I have seen children write with more precision.'

'You have missed your calling, Darcy. You should have

been a schoolmaster. Do you wish to continue the lecture or shall we take a ride in the park?'

We took a ride in the park. I learned they had all been to Bath because Mr Hurst had been advised by his doctor to drink the waters. 'Horrible stuff,' said Bingley cheerfully, 'but they say it does wonders for the system.'

'And how did you amuse yourself whilst Mr Hurst was drinking the waters?'

Bingley looked more cheerful than he had since his removal from Netherfield. He talked of his excursion, of the people he had met, but if he had found himself admiring any of the ladies he mentioned, I could detect nothing of it from his manner.

Now I was confused, wondering if he was, at last, recovering from his attachment to Jane Bennet. I could not think it would be wise to restore him to the lady, if that was the case.

I knew there was also the likelihood of Jane Bennet recovering from her attachment to Bingley. Had I been able to observe the lady for myself, I might discover the present state of her feelings. But my own situation left me with no alternative other than to stay away from Hertfordshire. I could not inflict myself on Elizabeth and I had grave reservations about sending Bingley to Netherfield alone.

I told Bingley I had seen Elizabeth in Kent, explaining how it had come about. He asked how she was, and had I enquired after her family? He did not ask if she had said anything particular about Jane, although he might have done so, had we not been hailed by some acquaintance at that moment.

The whole matter became a fresh source of vexation to me.

I could not determine what to do for the best, but I knew that doing the wrong thing would be worse than doing nothing at all. In my prayers, I asked the Lord for guidance and though none was immediately forthcoming, I felt better, for I could not feel He would wish me to continue in error, when I myself so desperately wished to do right.

In June, our whole party went to Eastbourne. Whilst we were there, we received news that a new Fitzwilliam had been born: Fitzwilliam George Fitzwilliam, grandson of my uncle, the Earl of Matlock, son of my cousin, the viscount.

The christening was to be held in July, in the private chapel at my uncle's country seat in Cromford, Derbyshire. I, along with my cousin Fitzwilliam, was asked to stand as godfather to the infant.

Plans were made accordingly: we would all travel northward together as far as Nottingham, where the Bingleys would visit their aunt. Georgiana and I would go on to Cromford for the christening. Later, they would join us at Cromford before we went on to spend the rest of the summer at Pemberley.

We returned to London two days before we began our journey, and there I found a letter from Lady Catherine awaiting me.

Mrs Collins was now telling my aunt all the news from Hertfordshire. It was disconcerting to find I had a source of information about Elizabeth, who was now taking a tour of the Lake District with some people called Gardiner.

I wondered about the Gardiners, for the name was unknown to me: they were not a family I had met in Hertfordshire. No doubt they were some of her friends and I was pleased for her because I knew she would enjoy the Lakes.

For myself, it was a fresh source of sadness. I found myself wishing I could have taken her there, thinking how wonderful it would be to watch her expression as I showed her Windermere, Coniston Water and the rest. We could have taken a boat and —

I stopped, reproving myself for indulging in vain wishes and was then struck by another frustration. Were I not now obliged to attend this christening, I could have taken the opportunity to persuade Bingley back to Netherfield. I could have restored him to his Jane and taken myself out of the way before Elizabeth returned.

I groaned: Fitzwilliam George Fitzwilliam could not have timed his advent more unfortunately.

We arrived in Cromford at the appointed time. Whilst Georgiana and Mrs Annesley cooed over the baby, Fitzwilliam and I walked up the hillside to Black Rocks, an outcrop of millstone grit where we had sometimes played as boys. We seated ourselves on the smooth flat top and, careless of our own safety, allowed our feet to dangle over the eighty-foot drop. A breathtaking view of the whole valley was spread out before us.

'Georgiana is looking well,' observed Fitzwilliam. 'And you, sir, are not. You are out of spirits and you have lost weight. What is wrong with you, Darcy?'

'I am not ill,' I said, 'and neither am I starving.'

'I am to mind my own business, I take it?'

'There is nothing wrong with me; I am perfectly well.'

Fitzwilliam gave me a doubtful look, but did not pursue the subject. 'So, you plan to move on to Pemberley next week?'

'Yes. Bingley and his sisters will join us. Can I persuade you to come and make one of the crowd? You would be very welcome.'

'No, I thank you. I must rejoin my regiment, I have been away long enough. We are encamped at Brighton for the summer.' He grinned at me. 'Do you wish me to give your regards to our mutual friend?'

'I beg your pardon?'

'Colonel Forster's regiment is there, also. Wickham will have a nice surprise when he sees me, will he not?'

'I had forgotten that.' I could not help but feel relief that he was removed from Meryton and unlikely to trouble Elizabeth again. 'No, Fitzwilliam, I send no regards to Wickham.'

'I shall speak to his colonel at the earliest opportunity,' Fitzwilliam promised me. 'I do not think Forster is the man to resent a hint. Wickham may find army life a little harsher than he has, hitherto.'

With this happy thought, we made our way homewards.

The christening took place: my godson screamed his disapprobation. Fitzwilliam left for Brighton the next day, and Bingley's party joined us later in the week.

One morning Bingley was struck by a memory. 'You promised to show us the petrifying wells, Darcy, when next we came into Derbyshire. Did you not say there was one at Matlock?'

Georgiana and Mrs Annesley exclaimed their enthusiasm for the excursion: a carriage was ordered and off we went.

Matlock is but a short distance from Cromford, and the journey was soon accomplished. More interesting than the spring itself was a display of 'petrified' objects, including kettles, spoons, scissors, even spectacles. My companions were delighted: I found some pleasure in watching their faces.

Outside again, I chanced to look ahead towards a group of people who were just moving around a turn in the road.

I could have sworn I caught a glimpse of a bonnet that I recognized.

It was gone before I could be sure, but I gave a shout and ran after it, pausing at the spot where it had disappeared, looking round frantically. It was nowhere to be seen.

I returned to my companions, feeling foolish. 'I thought I saw someone I know.'

I chided myself all the way back to Cromford. Elizabeth was in the Lake District; there must be hundreds of ladies who wore blue bonnets with a pink trim; and lastly, even had it been Elizabeth, which, of course, it was not, but even had it been she, what had I intended to do?

The incident unsettled me. I found myself dwelling on the possibility that Elizabeth, owing to some alteration in her plans, might, indeed, be here in Derbyshire.

It was, I knew, a notion born of my own desires, a little seed of hope, where there could be no hope. Elizabeth was in the Lake District. I must accept it.

My struggles were not assisted by the attentions of Miss Bingley and, once again, I craved solitude. When I received a letter from my steward outlining several matters of business, I made that my excuse: I would have a day to myself; I would leave for Pemberley ahead of the others.

So, Tuesday morning found me setting off on Starlight, a pleasant-natured, broad-backed mare: not a speedy mount but I was in no hurry. I took the bridle path through Via Gelia, riding at an easy canter, not thinking much, just enjoying the peace of the countryside.

I arrived in Youlgreave by ten. A little later, I passed the ancient stone circle at Arbor Low and half a mile further on I turned northwards again, towards Pemberley.

Four miles from home, I noticed Starlight beginning to peck a little to one side. Dismounting, I discovered she had cast a shoe. There was but one thing to be done. Half a mile to the east lay the town of Lambton and the nearest smithy.

I led the mare over the hill. As I looked down, I saw an open carriage bowling along the coach road towards Pemberley.

Once again, I thought I caught a glimpse of a bonnet that I recognized.

I caught my breath and swallowed. It could not be so, I told myself sternly. I had been through this before. Although Pemberley was open to the public view, no one was less likely to visit my home than Miss Elizabeth Bennet.

An hour later, Starlight freshly shod, I resumed my journey. As sometimes happens in the heat of summer, there was a swift, sudden downpour of rain, shortlived but drenching. I grimaced as I felt the dampness penetrate my clothing, but I forgot my discomfort at my first sight of Pemberley.

Over the amber-coloured stone of the buildings, a perfect rainbow arched the sky and, in the watery light, the house seemed suspended in another dimension, shimmering with an unreal, almost magical quality.

I reined in and stared silently as a strange, dreamlike feeling took hold of me, as though the earth was holding its breath, as though time was standing still.

Gradually, the illusion faded in the sun. Starlight whinnied, and I again became aware of discomfort from my damp clothes. I rode on. In the stable yard, I handed the mare to a groom and turned towards the house.

Then I started, for a moment believing myself in the grip of another illusion: I had caught sight of a bonnet that I recognized.

This time, it was no illusion; this time, I could be in no doubt; this time, I beheld the beloved face.

The beautiful dark eyes were regarding me in consternation and dismay.

Eleven

———

SO THERE I STOOD IN ALL MY PRIDE AND TERROR, trying to behave in a gentleman-like manner.

I asked many silly questions. I am embarrassed, now, to recall how foolish I must have seemed.

I asked after her parents; I asked when she had left Longbourn; I asked after her sisters; I asked how long she had been in Derbyshire; I asked after her family; I asked where she was staying; I asked after her parents; I asked how long she was staying.

I stopped myself asking after her relations for the fifth time, but I could think of nothing more to say: I could only recall, stupidly, that she was supposed to be in the Lake District.

My skin burned with a heat that had nothing to do with the July sun, for it was impossible not to recall our last disastrous encounter at Hunsford Parsonage. Elizabeth was looking as uncomfortable as I felt. Something in her eyes told me she was wishing I was miles away and I, unable to find any way of smoothing over the awkwardness of such a meeting, could only excuse myself and leave her.

I walked to the house in a daze. Once inside, I knew I could not let her go away without making some attempt to improve the situation. A miracle had occurred and I was not going to question it: she was here, at Pemberley!

Had we met by chance, in any other place, I could approach her only to pay the briefest courtesy. Here, I could join her as her host, and I could, without impropriety, offer her every civility in my power.

I ran through the house, scattering servants in all directions as I called for hot water, towels, clean linen, fresh clothes. By the time I reached my dressing-room, a footman was waiting to ease off my boots and my valet was there, stropping my razor.

I stopped and stared at him. 'I thought I left you in Cromford?'

'No, sir.'

I did not, as I might have done in other circumstances, demand to know how he compassed it. Elizabeth was here, and I had no thought for any other thing.

Hot water arrived whilst I was stripping, fresh clothes were laid out as I washed and my valet forestalled my arguments about not shaving by showing me my face in a looking glass. Cursing my beard, I submitted to the razor.

He was mercifully quick: ten minutes later, I was ready at last and on my way to meet my beloved.

I had left Hunsford Parsonage in anger, resentment and bitterness. There had been frost between us when we met briefly the next morning and I had no means of knowing how she had reacted to my letter.

But she was here: she had come with her friends, most likely because they had desired it, simply to view and leave again. I would wager Pemberley itself that she had been assured of my absence before she consented to the scheme.

A miracle! Something had caused an alteration in her plans to visit the Lakes; I had left Cromford a day early; we had both arrived at Pemberley on the same day and if that was not amazing enough, we had actually encountered each other; had I been ten minutes earlier or later, I might not have seen her at all. She could have been here, quite easily, without my knowledge.

A miracle, indeed. But one can expect only so much from miracles. What I had in mind, I know not. I think I hoped to show her I was not so mean as to harbour that first resentment. I think I hoped to obtain a little forgiveness for myself by showing her that her reproofs had received attention. I think I hoped to find some means of preserving the acquaintance and, in time, lessen her ill opinion of me.

I did not dare to hope for more.

I knew my gardener would have taken her party on the usual visitor's walk through the park, and by now they would be some distance from the house. Eventually, I spotted them on the other side of the river and made my way to the bridge.

Elizabeth had seen me coming, as I had known she would. She immediately addressed me in praise of Pemberley, then some unlucky thought crossed her mind and she flushed and fell silent.

Her companions were standing a little way behind. 'Will you do me the honour of introducing me to your friends?' I asked.

Elizabeth looked surprised; she quickly recovered; a fleeting glimmer of humour flickered in her eyes and was immediately repressed. In a very proper and sober manner, she introduced me to her Cheapside relations.

Elizabeth, I knew, was recalling the way I had so openly disdained these people in our last scene at Hunsford Parsonage. Trying not to begrudge her triumph, I now offered them my most respectful bow.

I do not think I managed to conceal my surprise. For this gentleman regarding me with friendly intelligent eyes was brother to Mrs Bennet, and I saw at once that he was wholly unlike his sister. Mrs Gardiner, an elegantly dressed woman of pleasing appearance, appraised me critically for a moment before favouring me with a smile of exceptional warmth.

I liked them, immediately. Whatever their condition in life, both Mr and Mrs Gardiner were people of good sense, good manners and good taste. As I turned back with them, Mr Gardiner engaged in conversation most readily, whilst Mrs Gardiner walked a little ahead with Elizabeth.

Since we were by the river, it was natural that our talk should turn upon fishing. It soon became clear Mr Gardiner was a keen angler and I was pleased, because this meant I could invite him to fish my river as often as he chose whilst he was in the neighbourhood. I offered to supply him with tackle and point out those parts of the river where there was usually the best sport.

He was clearly astonished by the invitation and I, looking ahead, saw his wife turn an equally astonished gaze upon Elizabeth. How that lady felt, I know not. The bonnet concealed her countenance from me.

Elizabeth, I was persuaded, held this uncle and aunt in the warmest affection. Yet their presence here, and their ease of manner convinced me they knew nothing of my proposal: Elizabeth had not confided in them. I thought it likely she had consented to visit Pemberley with them rather than do so.

I confess, I was glad of it. But, by their presence here, I knew Elizabeth must have spoken of me, most likely in terms of disapprobation. Mr Gardiner could not reconcile my invitation with whatever he had heard about my arrogance, my conceit and my selfish disdain for the feelings of others.

I had been justly reproved; I had been properly humbled; I had truly repented; I hoped I had improved: now I saw also that I had to live down my former reputation.

We all stopped to examine some riverside plant. Mrs Gardiner declared she was tired and her husband must lend his arm: I found myself walking side by side with Elizabeth.

I was delighted, but I was afraid, and far too embarrassed to know how to begin a conversation. Elizabeth spoke first. 'I believe your arrival here today was most unexpected, sir, for we had no notion of seeing you. Your housekeeper informed us you would certainly not be here until tomorrow; and indeed, before we left Bakewell, we understood you were not immediately expected in the country.'

She was clearly uneasy, in case I suspected her of mischief in coming to Pemberley. I quickly acknowledged I had returned early without informing my people. 'I had some matters of business to discuss with my steward, and so rode on ahead of the rest of my party. They will join me tomorrow.'

Now it was my turn to be uneasy. I knew what I wanted, yet before I could ask, I had to tell her who was coming and, in doing so, remind her of her worst grievance against me. 'Among them,' I said, 'are those who would claim an acquaintance with you. Mr Bingley and his sisters.'

I was scorching: I knew her thoughts had been driven back to the time when Bingley's name had been last mentioned between us. She wore her blank-faced expression and answered only with the slightest of bows.

'There is another person in the party,' I added quickly, 'who particularly wishes to be known to you.' With the whole of present and future depending on her answer, I went on to ask if I might introduce Georgiana to her during her stay in Lambton.

Elizabeth looked surprised, but agreed to it immediately. I felt like a man who had been given a reprieve.

I could not be certain Elizabeth had immediately grasped the implications: she had seen I intended a compliment, of course. My most pressing motive, however, had been to preserve the acquaintance between us: Elizabeth, had she but known it, had just given me permission to see her again.

We walked on, in silence. Elizabeth was deep in thought, but did not seemed displeased with her reflections. Saving my own reflections until later, I emptied my mind of all thought and determined to enjoy these moments of her company, and be as happy as I could. And so, for a heartbreakingly short time, I walked along the riverbank with my love by my side and the air was fragrant with the scent of meadowsweet and alive with the humming of bees.

When we reached the carriage, I asked Elizabeth if she would come to the house. She said she was not tired and so we stood together on the lawn as we waited for Mr and Mrs Gardiner to join us.

They had lagged a long way behind and were moving slowly, with Mrs Gardiner leaning heavily on her husband's arm; it would be some time yet before they reached us. There was time to talk, and I stole a wary glance at Elizabeth, wondering how much I could say.

She immediately made it clear she wanted no talk of a personal nature by beginning a recital of the places she had seen on her travels; perhaps she was right. After all, whatever I said would only mean I loved her and I was sorry for the way I had behaved. The first she knew, the second she might easily guess: I could not flatter myself she would be interested.

So I listened and made appropriate responses whilst she told me all about Matlock and Dovedale. When she had exhausted these subjects I began to tell her of other parts of Derbyshire, of more secret places with secretive names. I talked of Lathkill Dale which runs from Monyash, below Over Haddon, through to Alport, of the Goyt Valley, of Harrington and Beresford Dale, of Tissington and Eyam and Hope, of Edale and Kinder Scout.

If anything I said sharpened her interest in my county, I was doing myself no harm.

The Gardiners joined us and I was disappointed but not surprised when they declined my invitation to come to the house and take some refreshment. I handed the ladies into the carriage, we parted with civility, and I watched them drive away.

I walked slowly back to the house as I tried to sort out my impressions. Neither of us had been easy: that was impossible. But I could congratulate myself on having done something to lessen the embarrassment Elizabeth had displayed on being discovered at Pemberley and she had seemed pleased when I asked her to meet Georgiana.

Ahead, I knew, lay other awkwardnesses: it would be some time before either of us could meet with tolerable ease.

At least another meeting was arranged. Tomorrow, I would take my sister to visit Elizabeth. Georgiana would be embarrassed and shy, as she always was with strangers, but I thought Elizabeth and the Gardiners between them would overcome that.

The situation was too delicate to have high expectations, but I could renew my fishing invitation to Mr Gardiner. I could hope Elizabeth and the Gardiners would accept an invitation to dine at Pemberley; I could hope we might later plan an excursion. Perhaps, even though I hardly dared to hope this much, I might persuade her to stay on with us at Pemberley when her uncle and aunt returned home.

I knew my wishes were outrunning what I could hope. I knew I must exercise the greatest restraint. I could offer every civility, but I could not embarrass Elizabeth with any display of undue regard. She would know she had the power to bring on a renewal of my addresses, should she so wish it: and if, by some miracle, she should so wish it, she would know how to deal.

'. . . *you were the last man in the world whom I could ever be prevailed on to marry.*'

I winced as I recalled her last, contemptuous broadside. Was it possible to overcome such deeply rooted dislike? Yet I had to make the attempt, whatever pain was awaiting my failing in the endeavour.

For the moment, I could not help but rejoice. She was here, we had met; I would see her again. Compared with this time yesterday, my prospects were rosy indeed.

The following day when my party arrived at Pemberley, I did not immediately inform them of Elizabeth's presence in the neighbourhood. I had no desire to hear Miss Bingley and her sister delivering their opinions of her; still less did I wish for Georgiana to hear them. So we talked of commonplace matters as we sat down to a late breakfast and when the meal was over we waited for Georgiana to excuse herself, as we knew she would, by saying she must practise her music.

Four of us smiled at each other and silently rose to follow.

Mrs Annesley looked puzzled, but came with us. We entered the music-room to see Georgiana staring with incredulous delight at the instrument I had sent down for her.

'Good heavens!' exclaimed Bingley, teasing her. 'How did that get here?'

Half laughing, half crying, Georgiana came to hug me. 'Sir, never have I seen such a beautiful instrument. You should not; it is too much. I do not deserve it.'

'Shall I then give it to our cousin Anne?' I suggested, which produced an indignant squeal.

She obligingly played a few airs for us, then settled down to serious practise. She was still running though arpeggios an hour later, when I rejoined her.

'Come,' I said. 'Enough,' I produced a scarf from my pocket, and tied it around her eyes, blindfolding her.

She giggled but did not protest. 'Sir, what are you doing?'

'Come.' I led her through the house until we reached the sitting-room I had lately had fitted up for her. 'Another surprise,' I said, removing the blindfold.

'This is too much,' she said. 'Such elegance! Sir, you are far, far too generous.'

'Then you like it?'

'How could anyone not like it?' She wandered round, touching various objects and exclaiming her delight. 'It is beautiful. You are so good to me.'

I took a deep breath. 'Georgiana . . . er . . . do you remember hearing me mention a lady named Elizabeth Bennet?'

She had been examining a chiffonier. Now she straightened and turned to look at me, her eyes wide with surprise. 'She is the Hertfordshire lady whom you . . . er . . . the lady who was staying with the Collinses when you were in Kent, last Easter.'

'Yes. Well, now she is in Derbyshire.' I explained she was taking a summer tour with her aunt and uncle. 'At present, they are staying in the inn, at Lambton. I happened upon them yesterday, quite by chance. I remembered you said you would like to meet her, and you would, would you not? I am persuaded you will like her! I have promised to introduce you . . . Georgiana? My dear, whatever is the matter?'

To my absolute astonishment, Georgiana's face turned as red as fire and she looked away in discomfort. For some reason, she was now extremely reluctant to meet Miss Bennet.

'Georgiana, what is wrong?'

It took some time and some patience to persuade her to reveal her reasons. Eventually, I discovered she had once applied to Miss Bingley for information about Elizabeth.

'Sorry I am to say it,' I told Georgiana, 'but you cannot trust either of Mr Bingley's sisters on the subject. I promise you, you will find Miss Bennet both lovely and amiable.'

'How can I, when I know she must think ill of me?' cried Georgiana.

'Think ill of you?' I was all astonishment. 'Why should she? Georgiana, what has Miss Bingley been telling you?'

It was not Miss Bingley I had to thank for that: it was our cousin, Colonel Fitzwilliam. Knowing she must distrust either my opinion or Miss Bingley's, Georgiana had, during our stay at Cromford, also applied to Fitzwilliam for an opinion of Elizabeth Bennet.

My sister had perceived much more than I thought. Neither she nor Fitzwilliam would force my confidence, but upon sharing their information, they must have reached some conclusions: I had a particular interest in Elizabeth and something had gone awry.

Recalling our last day at Rosings, Fitzwilliam had ventured an opinion on the subject. It had something to do with Wickham, he supposed, and he had told Georgiana how I had revealed to Elizabeth all my dealings with that gentleman, including the story of her own planned elopement.

Georgiana was now deeply distressed because her indiscretion was known to Elizabeth.

'Why did you tell her?' she asked tearfully.

'I had many reasons. I am sorry, my dear, I had no wish to distress you. You may be sure the story will go no further: were I not certain of Elizabeth's discretion, I would not have breathed a word.'

'No. Fitzwilliam said so. He liked her, you know. He thinks . . .'

'What does Fitzwilliam think?'

'I . . . er . . . oh, never mind!' Georgiana looked down and began to smooth her dress with her hand. 'Very well, sir, I will meet her, if you wish it.'

I stood up, reached for her hand and kissed it. 'Just for half an hour,' I said comfortingly. 'It will not be too much of an ordeal, will it?' And when she shook her head and smiled,

I added, 'You will not object to riding in the curricle, will you?'

'You wish to go today? Now?'

'Of course. I have a pair of chestnut geldings I want to try out.'

'Ah! I see! What are their names?'

'Castor and Pollux.'

'The heavenly twins! How lovely.'

I sent word to the stables and both of us went to change. On our way out, we ran into Bingley. 'Hullo! Where are you two going so secretly?'

I felt my colour rise as I told him. Bingley was delighted. 'Lizzy!' he exclaimed joyfully. 'She's really here? Not five miles away? I must come, too. Wait for me, Darcy, whilst I change. I promise I will be quick.'

'You must follow us on horseback,' I said, telling him we were taking the curricle, which would seat only two. 'You know the way, do you not? I will tell a groom to saddle up for you whilst you change.'

In the stable yard, I gave instructions for Starlight to be saddled for Mr Bingley. With her turn of speed, I hoped we would be there for some time before he could join us and monopolize the conversation.

I handed Georgiana into the carriage, climbed in beside her, taking the reins and whipping up the geldings into a smart trot. Out on the coach road, I increased their pace, delighted to see the pair had a very respectable turn of speed. We arrived at Lambton within fifteen minutes.

Georgiana had grown silent and fidgety and, to own the truth, I was nervous myself. I reined in, handed the horses over to the ostler and helped Georgiana down from the carriage.

'We will be no longer than half an hour,' I promised and she nodded. Pale, nervous, looking as though she was going to her own execution, my sister resolutely followed me into the inn to be introduced to Miss Elizabeth Bennet.

Twelve

—⦾⦾⦾—

ELIZABETH VERY QUICKLY DISCERNED THE TRUE state of my sister's feelings and set herself to put her at ease. I heard the words 'music' and 'instrument' and 'my sisters' coming from Elizabeth and once or twice I heard a 'yes' or a 'no' from Georgiana.

I talked to the Gardiners about Derbyshire, enquiring about their holiday and asking them how they got on with the local dialect. Mrs Gardiner lapsed, briefly, into that vernacular and smiled at my surprise.

'I lived in Lambton for many years,' she informed me. 'This holiday is an opportunity for me to indulge my memories and renew some of my former acquaintance.'

A shy chuckle coming from Georgiana drew my attention

to that side of the room. I looked at Elizabeth, loving her more than ever for her gentle way with my sister.

When I looked back at the Gardiners, I saw they were watching me: by this time, I knew they must suspect my feelings for their niece.

I judged it time to give their thoughts another direction and told Elizabeth that Bingley was also coming to wait on her.

He came and made himself agreeable to all. There came a moment when both Bingley and Georgiana were occupied in conversation with the Gardiners and, to my astonishment, I saw Elizabeth watching the two of them, as though suspecting they might be attached to each other.

Only Bingley's sisters had entertained hopes in that direction: those two must have suggested to Jane a closer bond than really existed, a notion which had been passed on to Elizabeth.

I now perceived that, last April, she had believed my motives for detaching Bingley from her sister had been to secure him for mine. She probably still believed it was an additional motive.

There seemed to be little I could do about it. I could only wait and hope time would convince her I had no such ambition.

We stayed a little longer than the half-hour I had promised Georgiana, mainly because Bingley had so much to say. If he was hopeful of gaining some intelligence of Jane, he disguised his intention most carefully. He did ask Elizabeth whether all the sisters were at Longbourn, but I could detect nothing more than friendly interest in his expression when Elizabeth said only the youngest sister was away.

Before we left, I renewed the fishing invitation to Mr Gardiner, as I had intended, and a definite arrangement was made for him to join us at noon on the following day.

With a little prompting from me, Georgiana shyly invited them to join us at Pemberley for dinner one evening. Mrs Gardiner accepted and Friday evening was fixed upon.

Elizabeth remained silent: I had no means of knowing whether or not she was pleased by the invitation, but she smiled when Bingley expressed satisfaction at the certainty of seeing her again. He said he had still many enquiries to make after all our Hertfordshire friends.

I thought Elizabeth might interpret that as him wishing to hear more of Jane. But I, who knew Bingley far better than Elizabeth, could not yet be certain.

I had not forgotten that, should I restore Bingley to Jane, I myself might gain favour with Elizabeth. Anxious as I was to gain favour with Elizabeth, I knew I could not bring the couple together for my own selfish reasons: I had to be certain I was doing the best thing for them.

I could not tell. Bingley, who was used to wearing his heart on his sleeve, was, for once in his life, being quite insufferably circumspect.

On the way home, Georgiana needed my reassurance that she had acquitted herself well, and admitted she liked Elizabeth. She spent some time repeating things Elizabeth had told her, and I learnt the substance of their discourse.

With four sisters, Elizabeth said, it was a work of art to retain her own property, since gloves, scarves, bonnets and even bootlaces were borrowed without permission. Sisters, according to Elizabeth, were the most tormenting creatures.

'But the most diverting story,' added Georgiana, 'was when she described how her younger sisters arranged a treat for her which she then found she had to pay for.'

My sister seemed to be reviewing the visit with some satisfaction even though she had been constrained and embarrassed. I hoped Elizabeth had liked Georgiana: she had certainly exerted herself to please and had struck exactly the right note with a discourse which was general but lighthearted.

There were a few uncomfortable moments at dinner that evening, for then, Bingley's sisters learnt of Elizabeth's presence in the neighbourhood. Miss Bingley flushed and there was a glitter in her eyes which I did not like, but she contented herself with asking me if Miss Bennet's manners were still as impertinent as they had been in Hertfordshire.

'You must judge for yourself,' I said smoothly, 'for she and her aunt and uncle dine with us on Friday.'

This intelligence did nothing to improve Miss Bingley's humour. I regarded her calmly, determined nothing would ruffle my composure: perhaps she saw this, for she thought better of whatever she had been going to say.

Shortly before noon the next day, Mr Gardiner arrived to join our fishing party. It was peaceful by the riverside and most of the time we fished in companionable silence, but I, longing to hear something of Elizabeth, at last ventured to enquire how the ladies were spending their day.

They intended a visit to Georgiana, I was told. They were probably here, at Pemberley, at this very moment.

Mr Gardiner was getting along very well with Mr Bingley and Mr Hurst. I did not think he would mind if I excused myself and went up to the house.

The ladies were in the north saloon: upon joining them I was pleased to see Georgiana had not allowed her shyness to overcome her to the point of forgetting her duties as hostess: she had remembered to offer our guests some refreshment, and she was making a very creditable effort at conversation.

I doubt if there was one person in the room who did not suspect me of partiality towards Elizabeth. Mrs Gardiner and Mrs Annesley talked with Elizabeth, encouraged Georgiana to join in, and watched us. Georgiana exerted herself to talk, and watched us. Bingley's sisters made every effort to claim the attention of Georgiana and myself away from Elizabeth, and watched us.

Elizabeth saw them watching us and contrived to look unconcerned.

I know not whether I succeeded in looking unconcerned: I did my best, but I was anxious to forward the acquaintance between Georgiana and Elizabeth and did everything in my power to encourage it.

Caroline Bingley did not like what she saw. Choosing a moment when there was a lull in the conversation, she turned to Elizabeth with sneering civility and said, 'Pray, Miss Eliza, are not the militia removed from Meryton? They must be a great loss to your family.'

I felt Georgiana stiffen beside me, and I knew my own colour had risen. We both understood Miss Bingley's ill-natured attack had alluded to more than the behaviour of Elizabeth's younger sisters. She had meant to remind me of Elizabeth's acquaintance with Wickham, perhaps with the design of provoking me into disliking Elizabeth.

To be fair, Miss Bingley knew nothing of Georgiana's indiscretion, although my sister was painfully aware that Elizabeth did. I hoped Elizabeth's reply would not distress Georgiana.

Elizabeth struck just the right note of indifference. 'We bear the deprivation tolerably well, Miss Bingley.'

Thwarted in whatever design she had intended, Miss Bingley was obliged to subside. Georgiana began to breathe easily again and I felt a weight had lifted from my heart.

This was the first real indication I had that Elizabeth had accepted my assertions about Wickham. I knew not how quickly she had taken my word. But she had done so, and without consulting Fitzwilliam, which made that moment all the sweeter.

Our visitors took their leave shortly afterwards. As I attended the ladies to their carriage, I could, in Mrs Gardiner's presence, only refer to what had passed by saying, 'Thank you.'

She looked at me, understood well enough, gave a brief smile and shook her head. Nothing was said, but I felt it was the beginning of peace between us.

There was no peace when I returned to the saloon. I could see from Georgiana's expression that Miss Bingley had been giving vent to her feelings; now, she turned to me, telling me Elizabeth had grown brown and coarse since the winter. 'Louisa and I were agreeing that we should not have known her again.'

I kept my answer noncommittal and my tone discouraging, but Caroline Bingley went on at some length, criticizing every aspect of Elizabeth's appearance in detail. I watched her silently, thinking she should be made to stand side by side with Elizabeth in front of a looking glass, then she might realize the absurdity of voicing such opinions.

Having so far failed to gain a reaction from me, Miss Bingley then went on to remind me of some criticism I had made. 'I particularly recollect you, Mr Darcy, saying one evening, "*She*, a beauty? I should as soon call her mother a wit".'

I could not remember having said any such thing, but I could not deny it, either. There was a time, before someone had taught me better manners, when I would have taken pleasure, even pride, in making exactly that kind of snide remark.

'But afterwards,' continued Miss Bingley relentlessly, 'she seemed to improve on you, and I believe you thought her rather pretty at one time.'

'Yes, but *that* was only when I first knew her,' I said, since she was obviously determined to force me to speech; then I added, 'for it is many months since I have considered her as one of the handsomest women of my acquaintance.'

I left the room, left the house, not liking myself for giving her such a set-down: but if she thought I would deny Elizabeth for her sake, then she mistook the matter.

For all the attentions I had received from Miss Bingley, I was of the firmest opinion she felt no real affection for me. Her jealousy of Elizabeth and her designs on me were governed by her desire for connection and consequence, and, since I spent so much time with her brother, she must have believed she had a fair chance of success.

I had never encouraged her in such a belief, although I have to admit she had reason to take exception to my behaviour in this instance. In view of my scheme to separate her brother from Jane Bennet, my own pursuit of Elizabeth must now appear both inconsistent and hypocritical: had she been angry on those grounds, had she attacked me instead of Elizabeth, I would have respected her more.

For the first time, I wondered if Miss Bingley had really had the welfare of her brother at heart when she consented to remove from Netherfield. Even then, she suspected my feelings for Elizabeth, and might have been perfectly willing to sacrifice her brother to further her own interests.

It was an uncomfortable notion, but, I had to admit, not an unlikely one. I perceived it would not just be Bingley who would be acquiring unfortunate relations, should that union with Jane Bennet ever take place.

These reflections brought me back to the vexing question of what I should do about Bingley and Jane, and perhaps it was as well I was reminded of the situation or I might have missed the answer when it was presented to me later that afternoon.

I had returned to the fishing party by the river, pleased to discover my friends had enjoyed some good sport during my absence. Whilst we were engaged with our lines, none of us had much to say, conversation started only as we packed up our tackle, and Bingley began it by remarking what a happy circumstance it was that had brought Mr Gardiner to this part of the country.

The first part of Mr Gardiner's reply told us what I already knew: his business affairs would not allow enough time to follow their original intention of travelling as far as the Lake District. Derbyshire had been decided upon because Mrs Gardiner had lived here before her marriage.

He went on to say the shortened holiday was perhaps a blessing in disguise, and I, who had my own reasons for thinking so, turned to look at him in curiosity.

Mr Gardiner's reasons were not mine. 'It is the first time we have been away from our children for more than a week: my wife is missing them even more than she expected and, to own the truth, so am I.'

Until that moment, we had not known he had children. Answering our enquiries, Mr Gardiner informed us he was the proud father of two girls and two boys.

'And where are they at this present?' I asked. 'Who is caring for them?'

I realized what the answer must be even before I had finished speaking the question and, startled by what I knew was coming, I turned to look at Bingley.

'They are at Longbourn, sir. My niece, Jane, is looking after them.'

'Then they could not be in better hands,' I said absently.

Bingley was looking as though he had just had a vision of Heaven: Jane Bennet, on the sunlit lawns at Longbourn, surrounded by a group of little boys and girls. Even to me, the notion presented a pretty picture: I could easily comprehend what my friend was feeling.

Bingley's expression faded to be replaced by one of infinite sadness and I, shamed and distressed by the full knowledge of what I had done, could only look away.

I had prayed for guidance and now I had it, at least in the matter of Bingley's feelings. I had yet to ascertain the lady still favoured the gentleman, but there was someone who could answer that question not five miles away, at Lambton.

Fortunately, Georgiana was willing to indulge us with music that evening, for none of us had much to say. Bingley's sisters, perhaps a little offended by the events of the morning, talked of fashion with each other, but paid little attention to me. Bingley himself was quieter than I had ever known him, and my mind was occupied, not just with trying to determine a scheme which would restore him to Jane, but with another, more dreadful idea.

It seemed I had not wholly lost the habit of arrogance and conceit, for I had been presumptuous enough to believe the miracle of my meeting with Elizabeth had been for my own benefit and I had acted accordingly. Never once, until now, had it occurred to me the miracle might have been designed as an ironic answer to my prayers: I might restore Bingley to his Jane, yet still lose Elizabeth.

The plunging of my spirits as this notion took hold of me was enough to show me how high, how absurdly high, I had allowed my hopes to rise. I swallowed, trying to accept, but still I hoped a miracle for myself as well as for Bingley.

My own interests, however, must now take second place. First, I would do what I could for my friend.

The next morning I set off for Lambton on horseback, preparing myself for an uncomfortable interview as I went. I fully understood the impertinence of applying to Elizabeth for information on the matter of her sister's feelings, and I was perfectly sure I would have to bear some disapprobation. I could only hope my motive would persuade her to co-operate.

On being admitted into her presence I saw at once that any plans for Bingley and Jane would, once again, have to be postponed.

Pale, shaking, completely distracted, Elizabeth gave me no time to speak. 'I beg your pardon, but I must leave you,' she gasped. 'I must find Mr Gardiner this moment on business that cannot be delayed; I have not an instant to lose.'

'Good God! What is the matter?' I asked in dismay.

Elizabeth was in no fit state to tell me. Recollecting myself, I recommended her to send a servant after her aunt and uncle. 'You are not well enough; you cannot go yourself.'

She took my advice, but she was so distressed it was all she could do to make herself intelligible to the servant. When he left, she sat down, silent, pale and looking miserably ill. I offered to call her maid; I asked if she would like me to get her a drink, but she refused both these offers.

'No, I thank you. There is nothing the matter with me. I am quite well; I am only distressed by some dreadful news I have just received from Longbourn.'

She burst into tears and I, waiting in suspense, could only presume that illness or accident had befallen some member of her family. Picturing the worst calamity I could think of, I closed my eyes, dreadfully afraid her anguish was because something had happened to Jane.

At length, she found her voice. 'I have just had a letter from Jane,' she said, unconsciously relieving my mind of that fear, 'with such dreadful news. It cannot be concealed from any-one.' Between sobs, she went on to tell me that her youngest sister, Lydia Bennet, had left all her friends to elope with—of all people—George Wickham.

Never in my life had I been so astonished: of Wickham, I could believe anything, but I had understood him to be with his regiment in Brighton, removed from Meryton and the Bennet family.

'They are gone off together from Brighton,' said Elizabeth, unwittingly explaining some part of it. 'You know him too well to doubt the rest. She has no money, no connections, nothing that can tempt him to— She is lost for ever.'

In a choking voice, she began pouring out her own regrets for not having exposed Wickham as soon as she knew what he was. 'Had I explained only some part of what I had learnt to my own family, this could not have happened! But it is all too late now.'

I could understand why she had not: in the spring, when

she left Kent and returned to Longbourn, she must have quickly discovered the regiment was about to leave Meryton. With Wickham soon to be gone, she would have felt there was no point in exposing him. She could not have foreseen this trouble.

My mind seemed to be dwelling on trivialities. I found myself wondering what had happened to Wickham's heiress; I found myself wondering why Lydia Bennet had been in Brighton, neither of which was the most pressing question. I forced myself back to the main concern.

'I am grieved indeed,' I said. 'Grieved—shocked. But is it certain, absolutely certain?'

'Oh yes! They left Brighton together on Sunday night and were traced almost to London, but not beyond. They are certainly not gone to Scotland.'

'And what has been done,' I asked, 'what has been attempted, to recover her?'

She told me her father had gone to London and Jane had written to beg Mr Gardiner's assistance. 'We shall be off, I hope, in half an hour. But nothing can be done. I know very well that nothing can be done. How is such a man to be worked on? How are they even to be discovered?'

I shook my head. I knew Wickham well enough: I knew exactly how he could be worked on. The second question was occupying my mind, for I had no more idea than Elizabeth where he might be found. In London he would be very well concealed.

Someone must know where he was: I knew some of his

former acquaintance who, if they knew nothing of his present whereabouts, might direct me to others who did. It would take time; it would be a tedious labour, but in the end I would find him.

And, when I caught up with Wickham, I would make him wish he had never been born.

Thirteen

————

NOTHING I COULD DO, IN A SITUATION SUCH AS this, would make Elizabeth happy. Knowledge of her sister falling victim to Wickham would always be with her: I could only resolve the matter, and relieve her worst distress.

I blamed myself more than ever now for not having made Wickham's character known when I should have done so, last November, as soon as I found he had insinuated himself into Hertfordshire society. Had I taken Bingley's advice, had I spoken to Elizabeth then, none of this would have happened.

Elizabeth's tears had wrung my heart: I longed to enfold her in my arms, to comfort her, but I knew it would be infamous indeed to take such advantage of her distress.

To give my thoughts another direction, I had put myself to the task of devising a scheme by which I might discover Wickham. I had the feeling I knew something, something that would make everything easy, if I could but bring it to mind.

It had not come to me: I was too distracted by the sound of weeping. There had been an odd moment, in the midst of all her grief, when she had looked at me; a new realization had crossed her mind, causing her fresh anguish.

It pained me, too, for I understood only too well: she was now sorry she had been led into making me acquainted with the situation.

She saw, perhaps, the man who had so arrogantly expressed disapprobation for her family now being presented with fresh evidence of their folly and impropriety. She forgot, perhaps, my own sister had almost come to grief in the same way.

Yesterday, in ignorance of her sister's situation, she had comforted mine: now, the only comfort I could offer her was my absence.

I took my leave of her, assuring her of my secrecy and promising to convey her excuses to Georgiana for not keeping their engagement to dine at Pemberley.

She looked at me as I left, a look so heavy-laden with sorrow and grief I could hardly bear to tear myself away from her. Knowing I could be of more use to her elsewhere kept me to my purpose.

Whatever Lydia Bennet might believe, I was certain Wickham had not been induced to leave his regiment and flee Brighton for love of her. The real, more pressing, reasons for his flight would be very different: no doubt his creditors were becoming too demanding.

I could not help wondering if my cousin Fitzwilliam had increased Wickham's difficulties to the point where flight was necessary. It would be a strange irony indeed had his hints brought about this situation: but I could not blame my cousin. Wickham was Wickham, extravagant, wild, unpredictable and unstable.

By one of those strange coincidences that sometimes occur, on my return to the house, I discovered the post had brought a letter from Fitzwilliam. It began rather delicately, preparing me for some astonishing news, and went on to tell me what I had already learnt from Elizabeth.

Fitzwilliam's letter was rather more coherent than Elizabeth had been. Lydia Bennet, I now discovered, had become friendly with Colonel Forster's wife whilst the regiment was quartered in Meryton. Upon their removal to Brighton, the colonel had invited Lydia to accompany them as his wife's particular friend and companion.

I looked up from the letter, recalling what Fitzwilliam had once said about Colonel Forster: 'He was engaged to some silly little piece about half his age. I suppose he is married to her, by now.'

I nodded to myself, reflecting nothing was more likely than a friendship between Lydia Bennet and the colonel's lady.

Fitzwilliam, although hesitating to ask too many questions, had learnt that Lydia had left a note, proving there was no deliberate infamy on her side; she believed Wickham was taking her to Gretna Green.

Fitzwilliam had understood the connection between Lydia

and Elizabeth. He went on to remind me there was a miniature likeness of Wickham at Pemberley and suggested that, had I no objection to parting with it, it might greatly assist the Bennet family in their efforts to recover their daughter.

If Fitzwilliam had any suspicion I would involve myself more directly in the matter, he gave no hint of it. There were no other suggestions. I was glad to be reminded of the miniature, which had been painted for my father, for I had not thought of it myself. Certainly, it would be more useful than verbal descriptions. I would take it with me to London.

When I left Lambton, I had the hot-headed intention of setting out for London that same day: cooler reflection reminded me Elizabeth and the Gardiners would be travelling the same route. Having no wish to encounter them along the way, I resigned myself to waiting, merely sending a team of carriage horses ahead. I spent the rest of the day arranging affairs at Pemberley.

I left for London early the following day and reached my house in Eaton Place on Sunday evening.

As I travelled, I had time to think and after worrying the problem for some time, I knew the answer to the question Elizabeth had asked: 'How are they even to be discovered?'

I confess to the most dreadful feeling of revulsion when I understood who would have news of them. That same person who had been my sister's companion, that same person who had conspired with Wickham to betray me: Mrs Younge.

Every feeling revolted against applying to her for news of Wickham, but it could not be helped. I knew how rapidly he lost his more respectable friends: it was most unlikely that any other of his former associates would now have news of him. But she was of his own ilk, treacherous and conspiratorial by nature.

By the greatest good fortune, I happened to know where to find her, for somehow my valet had learnt she had taken a house in Edward Street and was now maintaining herself by letting rooms.

I considered the matter, and thought it quite likely I need seek no further. It would be natural for Wickham to go to her for lodgings.

I set myself to my task on Monday morning. I did not immediately repair to the lodging-house run by Mrs Younge; instead, I made a few enquiries in that neighbourhood, showing the likeness of Wickham, asking if he had been seen.

It was past four o'clock by the time I had some definite information: a tavern-keeper pointed out the father of a chambermaid who worked in Mrs Younge's establishment. He was surly and unfriendly, but a half-sovereign bought me a few minutes speech with the girl.

Yes, she had seen Wickham; yes, there had been a lady with him; yes, he had wanted lodgings with Mrs Younge, but all her rooms were taken. Mrs Younge had directed him to another part of town. 'No, sir, I am sorry, I know not where.'

So, I would have to see Mrs Younge. I took myself off to Edward Street directly, but the only satisfaction I had during the first interview was in my certain knowledge she knew where Wickham was, for she refused to admit even that much.

'You waste my time, madam, and your own, by these false assertions. I have it on good authority he has been here this last week. You have knowledge of his whereabouts and you would be wise to tell me. You do no one any service by withholding such information.'

'Indeed, sir? Am I now to assume you have his interests at heart?'

I wished she had known how ridiculous her smirk looked. 'You may assume whatever you choose, madam. You may be assured, however, I will find him, with or without your assistance.'

'Then I suggest you do so, sir, for you will hear nothing from me. I owe nothing to you, and he is my friend: I will not betray his trust.'

I might have set more store by this had not experience taught me the woman was ready to betray any trust, for profit. If all else failed, bribery would do the trick.

I only said, 'Then let us hope he will not betray your trust, though I fear it will be a long time before he can repay what he owes you.'

I saw the alarm in her eyes. She recovered quickly. She tried to deny it, but certain it was she had lent money to Wickham.

I said, 'Allow me to give you some advice, madam. You should not lend more money to Wickham than you can afford to lose, for you will be fortunate indeed, should you ever recover it.'

She glared at me. I smiled, happily aware that so far I had had the best of the encounter. I decided to leave whilst I still had the advantage. 'Think it over, madam. Determine for yourself how much loyalty you owe to Wickham.'

I left her, confident now. If other methods failed, I would, in the end, get what I wanted from Mrs Younge.

My other methods were tedious in the extreme and I pursued them for a while, merely out of my distaste for the idea of lining the pockets of that woman, but without much expectation of success.

It was late on Tuesday when I returned to Edward Street. By this time, Mrs Younge had remembered that she had always disliked me, a circumstance which troubled me not at all.

'Your opinions are noted, madam, but I venture to suggest they are hardly likely to influence anyone within my circle of friends. My opinions of you, however, could have far-reaching consequences, should I choose to make them known. A hint, perhaps, in Bow Street, could make your livelihood somewhat precarious, could it not?'

'There is nothing here to interest the runners,' she said loftily. 'I keep a respectable house.'

'Then you must value your reputation,' I answered smoothly. 'Indeed, I understand perfectly why you refused to take in Wickham. A good reputation is not easy to recover when it has been lost: a visit from the runners . . .' I shook my head and tut-tutted. 'Your lodgers would dislike it, madam. They would dislike it very much indeed.'

I will not repeat what she said to me. I let her run on for some time and she ran out of breath before I ran out of patience.

The woman was in difficulties: she would not have been so free with her invective had she not some reason to fear. It might be she had lent too much to Wickham and could not afford to lose customers, or there might be some other reason why she would fear the runners. I did not much care. My only reason for bandying words with her had been to conceal my own urgency for, had she perceived it, she would have been wholly impossible.

Now, it was time to suggest she might profit by giving me what I wanted. I said coldly, 'Your loyalty to Wickham does you credit, madam, but no service, when you must know he will neglect every interest but his own. I suggest you now consider your own interest. Something might yet be retrieved, for I am in no humour to continue my visits here indefinitely. I have more agreeable ways of spending my time. Name your price, madam.'

She wanted £500. I stood up to go. 'You will be more reasonable when you have had time to think it over.'

She had reduced her price to £300 before I reached the door. 'Sleep on it, madam. I will call again tomorrow.'

The next morning, after an hour of bargaining, with an occasional mention of the runners, I had Wickham's address.

I took myself there immediately. His landlady showed me into a parlour. 'Tell Mr Wickham that Mr Darcy is here and wishes to speak with him,' I said.

I was sorry I could not see what effect this message had on Wickham. The landlady returned to tell me he would be down directly. She regarded me shrewdly, offering me wine, clearly hoping there was profit to be made from attending upon a gentleman such as myself.

I did not disappoint her. 'I wish for privacy,' I said, producing a sovereign. 'Please keep other visitors out of this room.'

I received thanks and a blessing, which was more than fifty sovereigns had bought from Mrs Younge.

Wickham appeared eventually, looking seedy. He was nursing a sore head, I realized. However distressed he was for money, he had enough to indulge in wine. 'What are you doing here, Darcy?'

'I hope I am not wasting my time,' I said, regarding him with disfavour. 'You look very ill, Wickham. Could you not have shaved and brushed your hair? I doubt the girl still favours you as well as she might, if that is the appearance you present to her.'

Wickham pressed his hands to his temples and slumped into a chair. 'Must you talk so loud?' he complained.

'And I should not imagine she likes you when you are in your cups, either.'

'Damn it, Darcy, what do you want?'

'What possessed you to run off with the Bennet girl?'

'You cannot imagine I had any wish to be landed with that little doxy,' he said. 'She would come. I was obliged to leave Brighton on account of a few . . . er . . . shall we call them local difficulties?'

'I suggest you call them debts,' I said, 'since that is undoubtedly what you mean. Since you did not wish for her company, how, then, did she know you meant to leave?'

'Should I know? A man cannot be held responsible for what he says after a drink or two.'

'Do not take me for a fool, Wickham. You persuaded her into this.'

'She needed no persuading, believe me: she thought of it all by herself.'

'I do not believe you, Wickham, why should I? Never has truth been your strong point. Had you wished to leave her behind, you would have done so. I daresay the child had a little money, enough to assist your flight.'

'What business is it of yours?'

His behaviour taught me I had come pretty close to the truth. He had professed love for Lydia Bennet, persuaded her to an elopement, allowed her to believe he would marry her, all for the purpose of funding his own escape. He had done all this, had ruined her into the bargain and now he did not scruple to lay the blame for her flight upon her own folly.

'How do you live with yourself, Wickham?' I asked curiously. 'Do you never feel ashamed?'

Wickham was too full of his troubles. 'I had to do something,' he said defensively. 'You do not know what it is like to be distressed for money.'

'I confess I do not,' I replied, 'but do not expect me to be sympathetic. We both know how very little time it took you to squander your substance. If you are distressed now, you have only yourself to blame.'

'Oh, Darcy, what am I to do?'

'Do I know? I wish to speak with the girl.'

'What?' Wickham looked astonished. 'Why, for goodness sake?'

'Believe it or not, there are some who are concerned about her present situation. They have the quaint, old-fashioned notion it is not suitable. She is, after all, the daughter of a gentleman.'

'Why should you care? The Bennets are no friends of yours, Darcy.'

'There are some I may count among my friends. Summon the girl, Wickham.'

He complied more readily than I expected: perhaps he was tired of her already.

I had resolved to be gentle with Lydia Bennet, having assumed she would be shamed and embarrassed by her disgrace. I quickly discovered my mistake. She came, afforded me the briefest curtsey, and stared at me boldly. 'I know not why you should wish to see me, sir.'

'I have pledged myself to assist your relations, Miss Bennet, in resolving this present situation.'

'Why do you take the trouble?'

'Your family and friends have been greatly distressed by this elopement, particularly since no marriage has yet taken place. Why did you not proceed directly to Gretna Green, as I believe you intended?'

I knew Wickham had no intention of marrying her, but I was curious as to what she thought about it.

'Wickham had business to attend to here in London,' she said sulkily. 'It is of no consequence. We shall be married sometime: it does not much signify when.'

'What is Wickham doing about his business?' I enquired. 'Apart from drinking himself into a stupor whenever he can?'

I had hoped, by this remark, to give her pause and make her suspect the man she trusted was less than satisfactory. I was soon to discover Lydia Bennet did not hear anything she did not wish to hear. She ignored my last question, answering only the first.

'La, I am sure I do not know. Business affairs bore me. He knows what he is about.'

I talked to her very seriously, representing the disgrace of what she had done and the misery she had brought upon her family. She fidgeted, not from embarrassment, but from boredom. Nothing would persuade her to quit her present situation. I told her I would persuade her friends to receive her again and she declared she cared nothing for her friends. She spurned all my offers of assistance. She wanted no help of mine: she knew me for her dear Wickham's enemy.

Through her prattle, I learned of what I had been accused in Hertfordshire. It was as I suspected: I had overset my father's Will and deprived poor Wickham of the living at Kympton.

'Not that I care,' continued Lydia, tossing her head, 'for I prefer to see a man in regimentals. I cannot feel there would be any fun in being married to a clergyman, and so I told Mama when she was railing against Lizzy for refusing Mr Collins. Poor Lizzy! I am sure she was envious when she heard I was to marry Wickham. He was quite a favourite with her, you know.'

There was a triumphant note in her voice and I stared at

her, wondering if she understood how matters were with me. But she did not. Her pleasure was in the belief she had captured a man to whom her sister was partial. I knew Wickham was not above assisting this notion: how far her affection for him depended on it, I know not. Certainly, it pleased her.

All attempts to reason with her were in vain. She would not quit her present situation; she would not leave Wickham. Since she was resolved, I could only secure and expedite the marriage.

Marriage had never been Wickham's design, and when I saw him again, I did not immediately suggest it. Instead, I asked him what he meant to do now, pointing out that, since he had left so many debts behind him, he could hardly remain in the regiment.

He said he meant to resign his commission immediately. He did not know where he would go; he did not know what he would do; he knew he would have nothing to live on.

He was in absolute despair, which suited me for I knew that in such a situation he would be willing to grasp at anything. Letting him stew for a few minutes, I asked his landlady to bring us some coffee and waited in silence until it came.

'It seems to me,' I said at last, 'your situation would be benefited by marriage to Lydia Bennet.'

This solution found no favour with Wickham: he had other ideas. He meant to make his fortune by marriage, and was in no doubt his charms would tempt an heiress into matrimony.

I cast doubt upon his certainty. 'How many heiresses have slipped through your fingers, already, Wickham? Two, to my certain knowledge, and I doubt not there are others of whom I know nothing. You have a reputation, you know, which will not assist you in such ambition. Besides, in these circumstances, you are in no position to court an heiress. In fact,' I added, 'the way matters stand at present, you are more likely to find yourself in a debtors' prison.'

'You do have a bracing way of putting things,' he muttered.

'The girl is fond of you,' I told him. 'Heaven knows why, but she is. Mr Bennet is anxious to retrieve what he can of his daughter's reputation, and though I do not imagine him to be very rich, he must be able to do something for you. I would counsel you to forget your notions of a promising future and consider the prospect of immediate relief.'

'You have a point,' he admitted. I saw he was regarding me with a speculative look in his eye, but I said nothing. Some expense I would bear, and I suspected he knew it, but I had no intention of making him rich. After some reflection, he roused himself. 'Well, then, Darcy, consider me engaged to Lydia Bennet.' And he laughed.

'I wish you joy.'

'Shall we get down to business?' he suggested.

'No.' I had a sudden revulsion of feeling. 'I have seen enough of you today, Wickham. Tomorrow will be soon enough. I am leaving, now. I suggest you pay some attention to the girl: it would not do for her to change her mind, would it?'

I left, completely nauseated by the knowledge that I was assisting such a man to become the brother-in-law of Elizabeth.

I determined, then, to keep myself informed about Wickham for the rest of my days. He would never trouble Elizabeth if I could help it. Now I saw his future plain.

I would clear his debts; I would settle some funds, in addition to whatever portion she had, on Lydia. I would also assist him in his chosen profession, in a way that would please me far more than it would please him.

Fourteen

——⚬⚬⚬——

I RETURNED TO WICKHAM'S LODGINGS THE NEXT day, tipped his landlady another sovereign for the use of her parlour, and she brought coffee without being asked.

Wickham was not so obliging. I wanted matters settled quickly, for the less time I had to spend with him the better. But he was being superlatively stupid.

'Do you remember, Darcy,' he said, 'the time when we were lost in Peak Cavern, up at Castleton? I thought we would never find our way out.'

Boyhood memories would not soften me, and so I told him. He was determined to reminisce and went on, 'Those were the days. I was telling Lydia about the time we were snowed in at Cromford and took sleds into Via Gelia. And the time we went gathering those delicious chestnuts in Shining Cliff Woods, at Ambergate. Do you remember, Darcy?'

'Some of us have grown up since those days, Wickham. Since you are about to enter the estate of wedlock, you would be well advised to do the same.'

It was hopeless: he would go on. He talked of fishing in the Derwent, of meeting gypsies at Whatstandwell, of pony rides across Masson.

I stood up to go. 'I see your design, Wickham,' I said. 'You think recalling these memories will put me into a complaisant mood, so you might derive greater benefit. You will not succeed. I have more recent memories of you, which fill me with repugnance, and I know how you slandered me in Hertfordshire. You might have done better out of me had you'—I delivered the most cutting reproof I could think of—'had you behaved in a more gentleman-like manner.'

I left, angry with him, for the memory which haunted me was of Elizabeth, her eyes filled with tears, her slim shoulders braced to bear all the ignominy and shame of her sister's disgrace. Never, whatever the future held of pain or pleasure, never would I forgive him for that.

Meanwhile, acting on Wickham's behalf, although without his knowledge, I went to see a friend at the War Office and told him I wanted to purchase a commission in a northern regiment. Wickham meant to resign his commission in Colonel Forster's regiment, but he would have to do something, and, since his lady liked to see a man in regimentals, I proposed he should continue to make the army his profession.

My friend knew I did not purchase such a commission for myself, but he was in a jocular frame of mind and chose to chaff me about it. At length he was persuaded to be serious.

'Newcastle? Why Newcastle, Darcy?'

'It has the advantage of distance. And I know who the general is.'

'You do?' My friend gave me a speculative look. 'They say he frightens his own officers even more than he frightens the enemy.'

'Exactly,' I said. Wickham, although he did not know it, would find himself obliged to submit to a sterner discipline than any he had yet experienced. He would, if he was wise, exercise smartly when he was on parade and behave himself when he was not.

My friend said he would attend to the matter and advise me as soon as possible.

As a result of this, I was in a better frame of mind when I returned to Wickham's lodgings, and he, by that time, had made up his mind to be businesslike. Being Wickham, he wanted more than he could get. It took time, and mention of a debtors' prison, to induce him to be reasonable. Eventually, we settled down to serious business.

Too much time had been wasted and we did not finish our discussions that day, but by Friday afternoon, the business was agreed. He was willing enough to accept my suggestion to continue his profession in the army. It was settled. His debts would be paid, a sum of money settled upon Lydia and a commission purchased.

He saw the advantage of starting afresh in a northern regiment, where neither of them were known. 'You have the ability to do well if you apply yourself,' I said. 'You know how to make yourself popular. But I should renounce gambling, if I were you, Wickham.' By this time, I knew the extent of his debts. 'You are not good at it.'

Lydia pouted a little about leaving her friends in Brighton, but Wickham knew he could not return there and soon persuaded her she would make new friends in the north, assuring her there would be balls and parties, which was chiefly what she cared about.

When I left, Lydia was prattling about new clothes for her wedding and expressing her own satisfaction that she, the youngest of the Bennet sisters, would be the first of them to be married. Wickham smiled indulgently and said pretty things to her. I, disgusted with them both, was persuaded they deserved each other.

It remained to make Lydia Bennet's family acquainted with what had been done and with this object in mind I went to call upon Mr Gardiner in Gracechurch Street. He was not at home. Upon enquiry, I discovered Mr Bennet was with him, but was returning to Longbourn tomorrow.

I received this news with some relief. I knew not how far Elizabeth confided in her father, but whether he knew of my sentiments for his daughter or whether I was no more than a young man he met briefly last autumn, I wished him to know nothing of my involvement in this affair.

Accordingly, I postponed my intention of seeing Mr Gardiner until Mr Bennet had left. I left word, desiring Mr Gardiner to be at home when I called again, but I did not leave my name.

I returned to Gracechurch Street the following day. Mr Gardiner greeted me with some surprise and a great deal of warmth. When the usual civilities were over, I said, 'Before you left Lambton, sir, your niece made me acquainted with the matter which is at present causing your family some distress. It is for this reason I am here to consult with you. I have information concerning Mr Wickham and your niece.'

He became businesslike immediately, demanding to know the particulars. 'You have seen them both? And they are not married?'

'No, sir, they are not.'

'Could I expect it to be otherwise?' he murmured.

'But,' I went on, 'I venture to hope they soon will be. I have represented the advisability of marriage to Mr Wickham, and he has come to agree with me.'

Mr Gardiner was now regarding me with the liveliest interest. 'Mr Darcy, you astonish me.'

'Sir, I beg you will pardon my intrusion into the affairs of your family. But I had some knowledge of his acquaintance to assist me in discovering them.'

'You need ask no pardon, sir,' exclaimed Mr Gardiner. 'Indeed, I am indebted to you for your exertions on behalf of my niece.'

His tone left me in some doubt about which niece he meant.

'I confess, I felt I had a duty in the matter, also,' I said, 'for I neglected to make Wickham's character known when he first came into Hertfordshire. Had I done so, he would not have been received into society and this elopement would not then have taken place.'

Mr Gardiner was regarding me with some astonishment, but he said nothing and I, pained by the knowledge that I must lower myself in his esteem, braced myself to continue. 'I have sometimes been accused of pride and arrogance, and I expect you have heard something of it yourself, sir?'

'Indeed, I have,' agreed Mr Gardiner. 'I have, if I may say so, heard far more than I have been able to observe.'

I felt my cheeks grow warm, knowing who had spoken of it. 'I . . . er . . . I have lately been made aware of the evils resulting from such attitudes and never more so than in this matter. For I went expressly against the advice of a friend, who told me I should make Wickham's worthlessness known. I heeded him not, for I am not a man who cares to lay his private actions open to the world. My friend said sometimes it was necessary to prevent a greater evil. He was right. As we have seen.'

Mr Gardiner was examining his own fingernails with great interest. 'Mr Darcy,' he said unsteadily, 'you have persuaded me the whole business is entirely your fault. Indeed, now you have explained it to me, I can easily perceive that no blame at all should be attached to Mr Wickham or to my niece. I cannot understand why it did not occur to me sooner.'

Damn the man, he was far too perceptive. He might choose to be diverted by my confessions at present, but he would give me a hard time when he realized my design was to take the financial burden upon myself.

Before that happened, he expressed a desire to see Lydia and Wickham for himself. I had expected this, and had accordingly instructed my coachman to keep my carriage waiting.

The visit was brief. Mr Gardiner was stern, Lydia unabashed, with Wickham exerting himself to be charming.

'My wife,' said Mr Gardiner as we made the return journey to Gracechurch Street, 'has remained at Longbourn, but returns home later today. I am persuaded she will agree with me that Lydia should stay with us and be married from our house.'

'It will be to her advantage if you are willing to offer her your protection and countenance,' I agreed. 'And certainly it will be a comfort to her parents and sisters.'

'I am concerned more for them than for Lydia herself,' said Mr Gardiner. 'I declare, never have I been more shocked than I was by her behaviour, this morning. So far from being ashamed, she seems to be pleased with herself.'

'I am afraid she has been influenced by Wickham.' I excused her as best I could. 'She does seem to be genuinely fond of him.'

'So she may be, at present. I cannot feel there can be any lasting happiness for her in marriage to such a man.'

My own opinion was that each of them was as likely to be happy with the other as with anyone else. They were both shallow, extravagant and vain: lack of money was all that would cause either of them any grief.

Money became the subject of discussion between myself and Mr Gardiner as soon as we returned to Gracechurch Street. He perfectly approved of the arrangements I had made, confessing himself surprised only that Wickham had agreed to so little. 'My brother Bennet was convinced he would not take her for less than ten thousand pounds.'

'Wickham's present circumstances are desperate indeed,' I said. 'His demands are tempered by the necessity of immediate relief.'

He nodded, smiling. 'I congratulate you, sir. I flatter myself I am not without shrewdness in the matter of business, but I doubt I would have driven such a bargain with him.'

'Our long acquaintance has taught me his tricks and also some methods of dealing with them. Moreover, I object, on principle, to lining his pockets. I will do what is necessary, but no more than is necessary.'

At this point, Mr Gardiner discovered my intention of taking the financial burden upon myself. And I discovered just how shrewd Mr Gardiner was.

He insisted I had done much: he would not allow me to do more.

I repeated my assertion that this present evil was brought about by my neglect.

'The present evil,' said Mr Gardiner bluntly, 'was brought about by Wickham's perfidy and Lydia's folly and you know it.'

'It would not have happened had I not failed to make Wickham's character generally known.'

'As to that,' replied Mr Gardiner, 'it seems there were two

Bennets who also failed to make Wickham's character known. Jane, of course, hates to think ill of anyone and is always persuaded of unknown circumstances to account for anyone's misconduct. And, being Jane, she was convinced Wickham was sorry now, and anxious to re-establish his character: she thought it would be cruel to expose him. Lizzy, however, was under no illusions: she knew exactly what he was.'

I had expected to hear Elizabeth mentioned and was prepared for it. But I confess I blinked a little at this insight into Jane Bennet.

I said, 'Those ladies did not discover the truth until he was to leave Hertfordshire. I knew it when first he came, and should have heeded my friend's advice: he warned me there would be evil consequences in remaining silent.'

'You are not the only person who ignored good advice, Mr Darcy. My brother Bennet told me he was warned against allowing Lydia to go to Brighton. Lizzy did not foresee this turn of events, but she knew Lydia was ripe for mischief.'

This intelligence caused me some anguish on Elizabeth's behalf. She, the wisest and the best of the Bennets, would easily perceive the danger: and Mr Bennet would know she was right. In his indolence, he had ignored her.

Now, they both suffered for it.

I had to pull myself together. 'Had he known Wickham's character, she would have been protected from him.'

And so we argued the matter back and forth. Mr Gardiner was the most skilful opponent I have ever had to deal with. He reasoned with me; he tried to discompose me by throwing in an occasional reference to Elizabeth. He laughed at me, grew stern with me, grew exasperated with me.

I remained stubbornly insistent, though I confess I was exhausted by the time he ran out of arguments.

My respect for Mr Gardiner had increased a great deal during my battle with him, but I was, that day, glad to get away from him. He was too clever. He understood where my reasoning was specious as well as I did, and did not hesitate to point out the weaknesses and flaws in my arguments. In the end, I was forced to rely upon blind obstinacy to carry my point.

The next day being Sunday, I called again after matins. When I did, Mrs Gardiner was returned home from Longbourn. Between us that day, we agreed how matters should be settled.

Another argument ensued when I insisted the Bennets should know nothing of my involvement in the matter. Mr Gardiner knew his brother-in-law would credit him with providing assistance.

Eventually, however, he admitted Mr Bennet would feel less pain of obligation in believing a member of his own family had managed the affair.

I dined with them that evening and, at table, Mrs Gardiner's discourse touched on the situation at Longbourn.

Mrs Bennet had been of the firmest opinion that her husband had meant to fight Wickham, that in so doing he would be killed, whereupon the Collinses would take over Longbourn leaving the surviving Bennets homeless.

Foolish as Mrs Bennet was, she had real cause for anxiety.

'If only our dear sister would calm herself,' said Mrs Gardiner with a sigh. 'But she seems incapable of moderating her fears and her hopes. Poor Jane was quite worn down. Never have I seen her look so pale as she did upon our return to Longbourn.'

Miss Jane Bennet had been given authority to open her father's correspondence during his absence. Whilst Mrs Gardiner had been at Longbourn, a letter had arrived from Mr Collins, condoling with Mr Bennet on the severe misfortune the family was now suffering.

The content had not been revealed to Mrs Gardiner but, knowing the gentleman, I was not surprised to hear it had Jane shaking her head and Elizabeth spitting contempt.

Mr Collins heard all the Hertfordshire gossip from his in-laws, the Lucases. By now, my aunt, Lady Catherine, would be acquainted with the particulars. There would be a letter awaiting me at Pemberley, giving me her opinions.

On Monday, we made arrangements with our banks for the transfer of funds, and visited the rector of St Clement's, arranging for the wedding to take place in a fortnight's time.

Mr Gardiner sent an express to Longbourn, giving the Bennets an account of the situation. Mrs Gardiner collected Lydia from Wickham's lodgings and took her to Gracechurch Street.

Aware of neglecting my friends at Pemberley, I resolved to begin my return journey later that day. Wickham caught me before I set off and asked, rather awkwardly, if I would return for the wedding to act as groomsman for him.

I had not thought of it, and I said so. 'Surely someone among your acquaintance will suit the purpose better?'

'No, I do not think so.'

It had cost him something to ask me, I could see that, and I was, perhaps, more affected than I should have been. At all events, I agreed. 'Very well. I will return on Sunday week.'

When I recalled the distress he had caused Elizabeth, when I recollected how he had spoilt my design for restoring the happiness of Bingley and Jane, and cut short my own delight in Elizabeth's visit to Derbyshire, I thought I must have been mad in thus allowing myself to be softened into agreement.

I arrived at Pemberley on Wednesday, and found myself in some disfavour with my friend. Bingley is usually a good-tempered man, but he seemed offended by my desertion.

'Since your business was of such importance,' he said stiffly, 'why did you not attend to it whilst you were in town last month?'

'This business was sudden, unexpected and most pressing,' I assured him.

'Indeed? Of course, you had no need of my assistance?'

I smiled at him. 'Sorry I am to say it, Bingley, but in this matter you would have been very much in the way.' I watched him stiffen even more and added, 'I am not at liberty to confide in you: all I can say is that friends of mine were in trouble and needed help.'

'Oh!' Bingley unbent at once. 'What a fool I am,' he exclaimed. 'I should have known it was something of that nature. Darcy, I beg your pardon.'

'What did you think I was about?' I asked.

He flushed. 'I do not know what I thought,' he muttered.

I was curious, but since he was embarrassed I did not press him. 'The same business,' I added, 'will take me to town again next week, when, I hope, it will be concluded very speedily.'

Bingley was not the only one behaving oddly. His sisters were less attentive to me than usual, and I noticed my own sister eyeing me with some apprehension: even her companion, Mrs Annesley, was regarding me with some constraint. Something was going on, and I wanted to get to the bottom of it.

Not until the weekend could Georgiana bring herself to confess. Then I learnt that she and Mrs Annesley had been 'rather naughty, and she hoped I would not be very angry'.

I told Mrs Annesley she was old enough to know better. She blushed and admitted it, but Miss Bingley had been so very provoking, and she could not resist the urge to wipe the smile from that lady's face.

Mrs Annesley had told Miss Bingley she had heard a report of my engagement to my cousin Anne. She neglected to add the better information she had from Georgiana.

My sister, joining in the game, added, quite truthfully, that our aunt hoped the wedding would take place very soon. Georgiana had sighed, afraid we would be obliged to have Mr Collins conduct the marriage service.

'You should both know better,' I said. 'Mr Collins, indeed! Lady Catherine would demand no less a personage than the archbishop himself for such an occasion.'

Perceiving I was not seriously displeased, Georgiana

looked relieved. Mrs Annesley apologized and said she would, of course, correct the impression she had given Miss Bingley.

'I beg you will not,' I said, knowing Miss Bingley would make her suffer for it. 'You have done no harm.'

And, indeed, she had not. Miss Bingley, I venture to suppose, must have felt my admiration for any other lady would be overcome by the prospect of such increase in my connections, consequence, wealth and property.

I did not much care what Miss Bingley thought, since it had the effect of sparing me from her most irritating attentions. She was, in fact, better company because of it.

My own thoughts were frequently turned towards Longbourn and its inhabitants, wondering how they were faring now they knew the worst of their troubles were over, and wondering, especially, if one particular person in that household ever thought of me.

Fifteen

———

THE WEDDING OF WICKHAM TO LYDIA BENNET TOOK place at St Clement's as planned. It was a bleak affair, with none but myself and the Gardiners as witnesses. Only the bride seemed to be in good spirits.

Wickham informed me that as soon as the ceremony was over, he and Lydia were to proceed to Longbourn and remain there for a few days before setting off for Newcastle.

I was surprised, for Mr Gardiner's account of his brother-in-law's reaction to the elopement had led me to believe Mr Bennet would never receive the errant couple at Longbourn.

When I dined in Gracechurch Street the following day, I heard it had been brought about by the two eldest girls.

'Though I doubt they were consulting their own wishes,'

said Mr Gardiner. 'Meeting Wickham again would be the last thing either of them would want.'

Elizabeth and Jane, according to Mrs Gardiner, had, for their sister's sake, persuaded their father that Lydia should be noticed on her marriage by her parents. He had given them permission to visit.

'Those two girls,' said Mrs Gardiner dryly, 'credit their sister with the feelings they would have, had they been the culprits, though in my opinion Lydia wishes to go home merely to triumph over her sisters. She has no sentiment of shame: she thinks being the first to be married is a matter for self-congratulation.'

'I am surprised Wickham has agreed to go,' said Mr Gardiner.

'He will carry it off,' I told them. 'He will behave as though nothing untoward has happened. As he ever does.' I took the glass of wine Mr Gardiner handed to me. 'Wickham must know it would not be wise to have my part in arranging this marriage mentioned at Longbourn. But the girl talks without thinking. Can she be trusted to hold her tongue, do you think?'

'I left it to Wickham to persuade her,' said Mr Gardiner. 'Very skilfully he did it, too. But the truth is, she is not very interested in the part you have played and, therefore, she is unlikely to mention it. All she cares about is being married to her dear Wickham.'

With that, I had to be satisfied. Upon later reflection, I became assured Mrs Wickham would see no reason to mention my involvement, for certain it was she did not properly understand it. To her, I was just the man who had helped Wickham with some tiresome business affairs.

When I returned to Pemberley, the others had seen in the newspaper, as I had known they must, the announcement of the marriage between Wickham and Lydia Bennet.

My sister's naughtiness proved to have been a real blessing, for by it I was spared whatever derisive remarks Miss Bingley and her sister might otherwise have made. Only Bingley commented, saying Wickham must be truly in love if he had, in the end, made a choice so imprudent as to fortune.

'So it would seem,' I said.

My sister said nothing in presence of the others. Later, when we were alone together, she asked me if our aunt had made me acquainted with the fact of the elopement.

'She has,' I agreed. That lady's letter had spared me none of the details and had likewise made her opinion known. She obligingly informed me this false step on behalf of the youngest sister must be injurious to the fortunes of them all: 'For who would connect themselves with such a family?'

My aunt, had she known the answer, would have been most seriously displeased.

To Georgiana, I admitted I had known of it before receiving our aunt's intelligence. 'I hope you have not mentioned this to anyone here?'

'I have not,' said my sister austerely. 'But I thought you must know of it. It is the reason why Miss Bennet and the Gardiners left Derbyshire in such a hurry, is it not?'

'It is.'

'And she, I mean Elizabeth, she herself made you acquainted with the matter?'

'She did.'

Georgiana nodded to herself. I waited. I cannot disguise I
disliked the prospect of connecting myself with Wickham. I
disliked it, but I would not shrink from it, for now I knew the
pain of losing Elizabeth, and that was worse. Once, I had had
to bear that pain: I might have to face it again, for I was by no
means certain of overcoming her dislike; I was by no means
certain of winning her.

I only knew I would not let Wickham stand in the way of
my own happiness.

Georgiana, however, had reasons more complicated than
mere pride for disliking a connection with Wickham. It pained
me to feel she was about to voice objections of her own.

She did not. My dear, my beloved sister, put me to shame,
when she said, 'I was most disappointed when my acquaintance
with Miss Bennet was cut short so abruptly. I have been meaning to consult with you, sir, about an idea I had. I wondered if
I might write to her and invite her to stay with us, here at Pemberley? Mr Bingley and his sisters go on to Scarborough very
soon, but we do not have to accompany them, do we?'

She could not have spoken her approbation more clearly
and for a time I was too moved to do anything but hug her
and speak her name. Recovering at last, I told her I planned to
persuade Bingley back to Hertfordshire.

'It is better so.' I said, 'for many reasons. If you do not accompany the others to Scarborough, you will be left alone at

Pemberley with only Mrs Annesley for company. Will you mind?'

'I would prefer not to go to Scarborough,' admitted Georgiana. 'To own the truth, I am finding the society of Mr Bingley's sisters a little irksome, at present.'

I did nothing until I was certain Wickham had left Longbourn for the north. Knowing he must pass through Sheffield on his journey to Newcastle, when he was due there, I sent a servant to check he was indeed proceeding on his journey as planned. I wanted no more unpleasant surprises from Wickham.

Satisfied on that point, it was scarce the work of a moment to persuade Bingley to change his mind about accompanying the others to Scarborough.

Having accomplished this, I allowed some time to pass before asking him whether anyone had shown an interest in purchasing the lease of Netherfield. Upon being told no one had, I went on to express some curiosity about how our Hertfordshire friends were faring.

Bingley said nothing, but I was encouraged by his expression. At breakfast the next morning, I returned to the same subject and also mentioned the excellent sport we had there last year.

It was almost too easy. We sent servants to open up the house and a few days later we set off for Netherfield. There, with affectation of innocence, we went out shooting. Some of our neighbours visited: Mr Bennet did not.

On the third morning after our arrival in Hertfordshire,

Bingley represented to me how very impolite it would be should we neglect to wait on the ladies of Longbourn.

Faces appeared at one of the windows as we entered the paddock and rode towards the house. The two most earnestly sought did not appear, but I had no doubt they were by now well advised as to who was approaching.

How Bingley felt, I know not. I know my own mouth was dry as we were admitted into the presence of the ladies.

We stayed for half an hour and Elizabeth had little to say. She enquired after Georgiana, answered my own enquiries after the Gardiners and spent most of the time concentrating on her needlework. I noticed a few anxious glances at her sister, as though she expected Jane to be discomposed by Bingley's presence. There were no glances in my direction, or none that I could perceive. Whenever I looked at her, she wore her blank-faced expression which spoke displeasure.

Mrs Bennet did most of the talking: she welcomed Bingley with effusive civility, and myself with cold, ceremonious politeness. She began to talk of her daughter's marriage to Wickham, speaking of it with some pleasure, as though it had been properly arranged, unaware, I suppose, that either of us knew the truth of the affair.

Fortunately for him, Bingley did not, so he was able to respond to her chatter with tolerable ease.

I turned my attention to Jane Bennet. She was friendly, but not effusive, and not at all embarrassed. She appeared to be entirely unaffected and, when Bingley spoke to her, she chatted quite easily.

I did not know what to make of her. Had it not been for the

anxiety in her sister, I would have come to the same conclusion I had reached at the Netherfield ball last year.

I think I was watching her too attentively: she seemed to become aware of my scrutiny, looked up and smiled at me.

I will swear revenge was the last thing on the lady's mind. But she had it, in that moment. She was the one person in the world who had most reason to detest me, and she was the one, the only one, who showed me a little kindness at Longbourn that day. I felt all the meanness of my own behaviour towards her more keenly than ever before.

I hope I managed to return her smile: I cannot be certain I did. I know my colour rose, although I think that circumstance went unnoticed.

I was relieved when the half-hour visit was over, and we got up to go. Mrs Bennet, her hopes of Bingley now revived, invited us to dine at Longbourn in a few days' time. Bingley accepted the invitation for both of us.

Bingley was in good humour: he wanted to visit the Lucases, too. There, I received a warmer welcome. My aunt, after all, was patron to their in-law, Mr Collins, reason enough for their civility. Nevertheless, I felt a genuine spirit of goodwill was there, in contrast to the Bennet household.

It soothed me a little, but it could not console me for the cold reception I had received from Elizabeth, which was all the more painful for recalling how agreeable she had been in Derbyshire. It seemed she was determined to give me no further encouragement.

The Lucases invited us to dine two days after our engagement at Longbourn. I said I could not be certain of keeping the engagement, since I might be called to town on business.

'Darcy,' said Bingley seriously, on the way back to Netherfield, 'I think it is time you told me what is wrong. You have been going back and forth to town all summer, and now I hear you are planning to go again.'

I was silent. I could not tell him what had been taking me to town lately, and I could hardly inform him that, should I discover the nature of Jane Bennet's feelings to be favourable towards him, I meant to take myself out of his way.

He was waiting for an answer. At last, I said, 'I beg you will not ask any questions, at present, Bingley, since I find myself in some uncertainty.'

'That in itself is unusual.' Bingley shook his head. 'You are changing,' he said. 'I cannot quite determine what the difference is, but I know there is one.' He paused, seeming to make up his mind, then added, 'Tell me the truth, Darcy: is our friendship becoming irksome to you?'

'Never think such a thing!' I exclaimed. 'Indeed it is not! In fact, I—' I stopped, then added more slowly, 'I have come to value you more than ever, these last few months. There have been several occasions when . . . when I have wished I had followed your example . . . or taken your advice.'

He laughed, embarrassed, and more than a little surprised. 'This is a day of wonders, indeed! Never did I think to hear such words from you.'

'You are wiser than you know,' I told him. 'And, I admit, wiser than I have given you credit for, in the past.'

'Heavens above! You have changed even more than I thought.'

He spoke in a bantering tone, trying to lighten my mood, but fell silent when he saw he could not succeed.

When we reached Netherfield, Bingley discovered he had some letters to write and I, disturbed by this conversation as well as by our visit to Longbourn, took myself into the gardens.

Perhaps I should not have been quite so emphatic in my expression of regard for Bingley, for I suspected the day was approaching when I must forfeit his friendship. Having caused months of unhappiness by my presumption and interference, I could hardly expect to retain it.

His regard for Jane Bennet was as strong as ever. Should the lady betray any symptom of regard for my friend, my endeavours must be directed towards securing their happiness, whatever the outcome for myself.

From the Gardiners, I had learnt a little of Jane Bennet. It seemed she was truly as good-natured as all reports of her suggested, but without being weak. She would admit a mistake if she truly believed she had been wrong, but where she felt she was right she would remain firm. She was more patient, more tolerant than Elizabeth; she was serene and she was kind. I was persuaded she was exactly the right kind of woman for Bingley.

Whatever her feelings she certainly did not display them openly. In such a household, in such a neighbourhood, I could understand why she would not, but it made the task I had set myself seem impossible. I could only hope to catch sight of her in an unguarded moment.

I had, so far, resolutely avoided thinking of myself: I had high-mindedly determined my purpose was to see Jane Bennet and judge if she were still partial to Bingley.

I had other designs: of course I had. I wanted to know how far I dared to hope for success in winning Elizabeth.

If her behaviour this morning was a true indication of her feelings, it would seem there was no hope at all.

In Derbyshire, at Pemberley, I knew she understood my feelings, that I had been doing everything in my power to woo her. I had allowed myself a little hope, not expecting any swift results, but thinking I might obtain some forgiveness when she understood how bitterly I regretted my past behaviour, hoping she might overcome her abhorrence of me when she saw I had taken her reproofs to heart.

I had expected more time, for they had planned to stay in Lambton for ten days: in the event, they had stayed only three days, thanks to Wickham. At some point, during those weeks we had been apart, she had decided against me.

I brooded over Wickham, recalling Elizabeth's distress, her tears when I had come upon her that morning. As I reviewed that dreadful scene, I began to comprehend, with the most painful clarity, exactly what Elizabeth must now think of me.

I understood what she must have seen: the man who had so arrogantly disdained her family, once again returning to his former ways when faced with this fresh evidence of folly and impropriety; detaching himself from them, from their trouble, not lifting a finger to help.

What a fair-weather friend she must think me! All my former attempts to win her forgiveness and approval must seem worthless indeed in the face of such apparent desertion. Had she thought of me at all, Elizabeth must have imagined me strutting around at Pemberley in all my pride and disdain.

The result of these reflections sent my spirits into such despondency as I had never known before. Even when she rejected my proposals, she could not have thought so ill of me as she must do now.

This time, I could not explain myself, by letter or by any other means. I had purchased honour for Lydia Bennet, and my chief design had been to spare Elizabeth's feelings, but I would not have her know I had done it. I took no pleasure in knowing I had made Wickham her brother-in-law.

If Elizabeth despised me now, there was nothing at all I could do about it.

By Tuesday, when we set out to keep our engagement at Longbourn, I had reasoned myself into a slightly more hopeful frame of mind. I reminded myself I had only my own conjectures to account for that half-hour on Saturday: I would see how she behaved this evening before reaching any firm conclusions.

We were not the only company at Longbourn that evening: Mrs Bennet seemed to have invited the whole neighbourhood.

Jane Bennet gave herself away very early in the evening. As we entered the dining-room, Bingley hesitated, wondering,

I think, whether he dare take the place beside her. Jane looked round, smiled, and settled it. As he joined her, her colour rose and her eyes glowed, showing her delight.

I would have gladly sacrificed my right arm for one such look from Elizabeth.

Mrs Bennet asked me to take the place beside her: knowing how much the lady disliked me, I was surprised at the civility, but it was not one I could refuse. Now I was seated as far from Elizabeth as the table could divide us.

Later, when we gentlemen joined the ladies in the drawing-room, I discovered the ladies had crowded close to the table where Jane and Elizabeth were dispensing tea and coffee. There were no vacant seats; there was no space to bring up another chair. A young lady, no one I knew, was talking to Elizabeth. I was obliged to join the Lucases at the far side of the room.

She made polite enquiries after Georgiana when I took back my coffee cup. We were not left in peace for long enough to indulge in any more conversation, for that same young lady once again demanded her attention.

All seemed accidental, but I began to suspect a conspiracy. I have known ladies to request others of their sex to protect them should the attentions of a gentleman become an embarrassment. Well could I imagine Elizabeth speaking thus to a friend: 'I beg you, spare me, if you can, from the offence of Mr Darcy's notice!'

When the card tables were brought out, I was invited by Mrs Bennet to join the party playing whist. Elizabeth did not play whist. By this time, I was persuaded Mrs Bennet also understood Elizabeth wished to remain as separate from me as possible.

Whatever one said about Mrs Bennet, her affection for her daughters was real. For their own sakes, she wanted to see them married, and certainly she believed any marriage was better than none. Had she known of my sentiments, she would have acted differently: having no suspicion, knowing only that her daughter shared her dislike of me, she was willing to oblige Elizabeth. I spent the evening at a different table and I knew I had nothing to hope for.

I was thankful I had ordered our carriage to be early. Bingley was not. 'Why did you do that, Darcy?' he demanded. 'Certain I am Mrs Bennet would have invited us to stay on for supper had we let the others go first.'

'You cannot be hungry after a dinner such as that.'

He laughed, 'I would have forced myself to eat, all the same.'

'And let Miss Bennet think you a glutton?'

He caught his breath and was silent. In between his attentions to Jane Bennet throughout the evening, I had seen him direct one or two wary glances at me. He was hoping I had not noticed.

I am a much bigger man than Bingley: taller and broader. Whenever he referred to our comparative size, Bingley always laughingly declared he was afraid of me. Never before had I taken this seriously: now I perceived, however humorously spoken, there was some truth in it. I came late to the understanding that I had, in some measure, actually intimidated him into renouncing his love.

Neither of us spoke again until we arrived at Netherfield. Then, as we removed our coats, I said, 'Bingley, I must speak with you.'

'Am I stopping you?' When I did not answer he added, 'Very well. You mean business, I see. Though why on earth you had to—oh, well, never mind.'

He led the way into the library, clearly agitated, wholly misunderstanding my purpose. I followed, knowing he would understand soon enough, knowing the next hour was going to be very painful indeed.

Sixteen

———◆◆◆———

BINGLEY BEGAN TO TALK THE MOMENT I HAD CLOSED the door. Although he knew Jane Bennet was at present indifferent to him, he meant to do everything in his power to woo her and hope to win her at last.

'Er . . . Bingley—'

'I know what you are going to say, Darcy, I know you disapprove of her relations. I have tried to forget her but it is no use, I cannot. I am now determined. I should not have let you persuade me against her. I know you think I have been in love before, but I have not! Not like this, never like this! Oh, will you ever understand? You do not know what it is to be in love!'

He went on in this vein for some time. When at last I was able to speak, I said simply, 'You are wholly mistaken.'

He stared at me. 'How so?'

'I am not going to try to persuade you against Jane Bennet. I do understand, and I do know what it is to be in love.' And whilst he was struggling to comprehend, I added, 'There are certain circumstances in my own life, Bingley, which have made my interference in your affairs seem somewhat absurd.'

He shook his head. 'Now, I am all bewilderment,' he complained.

I went to stare through the window, looking out over the moonlit gardens. 'Can you guess what I did?' I demanded. 'Having decided last year that you should forsake Miss Bennet, having most emphatically represented to you all the evils of such a choice, can you guess what I then did?'

'Darcy, what are you talking about?'

'I proposed to Elizabeth,' I said.

An incredulous silence was broken at last by an incredulous laugh. 'Darcy—'

'Once you said should I ever fall in love, I would make myself ridiculous,' I reminded him. 'You were right. I have. Believe me, I have.' Having kept the whole of it to myself for so long, I found that once I had begun to speak of it I could not stop. I told him all that had happened.

Bingley was very surprised and very concerned. 'Never had I the smallest suspicion,' he confessed. 'Oh, Darcy, what can I say?'

'Nothing to any purpose,' I admitted. 'I am not the first man to suffer such a disappointment, and I doubt I will be the last. Forgive me, I had not meant to burden you with this.

My intention was merely to inform you of the circumstance which has proved my interference in your affairs to be utterly preposterous.'

He nodded, half amused, half attentive. I went on, 'I have never wished to do evil, Bingley, but I have come to realize that separating you from Miss Bennet was truly a wicked thing to do. For what it is worth, I am sorry now that I did.'

'You meant well, I know,' he said. 'It is not wholly your fault, for I have been thinking I myself should have been more resolute.' He smiled at me and when he saw there was no lightening of my expression, he raised his voice to a bantering tone. 'I think perhaps I may pardon you.'

'Perhaps you may not,' I said unhappily, 'for you do not yet know the worst of it. I have, in fact, been guilty of some duplicity. I will deceive you no longer: Miss Bennet was in town for several months last winter, from January through to April, in fact. She was staying with the Gardiners. I knew it and I concealed it from you. And I know, I knew then, I should not have done so.'

As Bingley took in this information his expression changed: his face became like a mask. At first he stood absolutely still, then he began to walk: he walked up and down the room, clenching and unclenching his fists and would not speak until he was certain master of himself. I waited in unhappy silence.

At last he said, 'And what excuse, what reason, do you have to give for this concealment?'

'My reasons, for what they are worth, were the same ones

I gave for separating you in November. At that time, I still believed Miss Bennet indifferent to you.'

'At that time —' Bingley became very still. I could perceive the implications were understood, but his countenance was still angry. 'Am I to infer from this,' he said coldly, 'that you have undergone a change of opinion on that subject?'

'I have, yes.'

He flung himself down in a chair. 'I find it astonishing,' he said, 'that having met with her only twice, as I have, since that time, your opinion can now be so altered. How do you account for it?'

I watched him carefully. Never before had I seen such a mood in him and I could do no more than give him my explanations. I told him I had learnt something of Miss Bennet from both Elizabeth and the Gardiners and had come to realize my previous judgement had been too hasty, based as it was on observation of her appearance alone, with no real knowledge of her character.

'I began to comprehend she was a modest lady, who would guard her behaviour and expression, particularly whilst in company of her neighbours. The Lucases mean well, but they are especially inquisitive, are they not?'

'Jane would not like to be the subject of gossip,' he admitted. 'Though I find this a very insufficient explanation for your reversal of opinion.'

'There are those who know her better than I. There have been hints that she was not as indifferent as I had supposed.'

'Indeed? From whom?'

'From Elizabeth, if you must know. And the Gardiners. I have been uneasy about my own actions for some time. I have said nothing until now, for I wanted to observe her for myself, to detect, if I could, some evidence of her true feelings. Tonight I did. Even the Jane Bennets of this world give themselves away, occasionally.'

'You cannot believe she cares for me now? Not after all this time, after deserting her, after all my neglect?'

'I am quite certain she does.'

'I wish I could believe it.'

It took many assurances on my part before he would believe it, but he was, fortunately, still in the habit of relying on my opinion. After a while he began to look happier.

At last I said, 'I shall take myself off to London tomorrow, out of your way. You will get on much better without me.' I swallowed, adding painfully, 'Bingley, I do not expect you to pardon my interference, after all the unhappiness I have caused. But I want you to know that I am truly sorry.'

I know not how Bingley could bring himself to forgive me: certainly, I could not have pardoned such interference as easily as he did. He was reconciled by his own observation that I had acted out of concern for his welfare and, upon discovering myself mistaken, I had taken pains to put matters right.

'Unlike some,' he added, 'who are no doubt still preening themselves over their part in the enterprise.' He gave a grim smile. 'Do not look at me like that, Darcy. I know others have been involved in this.'

'At my persuasion.'

'How much persuasion?' When I did not reply, he said, 'No matter. They shall answer for themselves.'

'Bingley,' I said in alarm, 'I beg you will not quarrel with your sisters. I am sure they thought, as I did, that it was for the best.'

'Best for whom?' He shook his head. 'I know my sisters, Darcy. They knew more of Jane than you did. If she cared for me last year, they knew it, whatever they professed to believe. They deceived me and they encouraged you to deceive yourself.'

'For what purpose?'

'I leave it to you to determine,' said Bingley.

Since I had already determined at least some part of their design, I felt it best, after exonerating Mr Hurst, to say no more.

I left Netherfield for London on the following day, but not before Bingley had extracted a promise of my return. He said he would write to me as soon as he had news to impart and grinned when I begged him to make his letter at least halfway readable.

I settled back into my carriage and began to take stock of my situation. I had fully expected Bingley to end our friendship as soon as he realized it had cost him almost a full year of happiness. Never had I been so grateful or so moved as when he held out his hand to me and said we need not mention the subject again.

In such a friendship I was truly blessed, I thought. It behoved me now to be certain that never would he have cause to regret his generosity. He would receive such assistance as was in my power and I knew some assistance, at least, *was* in my power: his brother-in-law, Wickham, might impose upon him for money, but I would make certain that gentleman did not become too ambitious.

I had not now the smallest hope of winning Elizabeth. After two meetings of such determined avoidance, I could no longer blind myself to the truth: she wanted none of me. I had to accept it, and rally my spirits as best I could.

During those first few days in town, I found my own company, which had in these last few months been so necessary, was now irksome to me. Such business as I had was quickly despatched. Few of my acquaintance were in town, but I visited those who were.

I attended the fencing school, went to the theatre, rode out in the park and wondered if the rest of my life was going to be spent in such aimless pursuits. I could not pass a shop window without seeing something I would like to purchase for Elizabeth.

On Monday, I received the expected letter from Bingley. He told me he was the happiest man in the world, and I believed him.

He had taken to heart my plea for a letter which I could read, and there was a postscript with which he had taken special care, telling me to make of it what I could. Jane, he told me, had been surprised when he mentioned our meeting with Elizabeth in Derbyshire, for Elizabeth had told her nothing. Believing herself in her sister's confidence, Jane did not know how to account for this.

I could account for it myself, though not in any way that brought me joy. There had been trouble in the Bennet household when Elizabeth returned: all other considerations would have been set aside. Later silence on the subject would be to avoid causing pain to her sister by mention of Bingley.

Elizabeth, I knew, would be delighted by her sister's engagement. Perhaps she would deduce I had played my part in reuniting the couple: I thought she would be pleased with me for that, at least.

In the days that followed, I visited my tailor, went to the races, watched a prize-fight, attended concerts: anything to keep myself occupied.

On Wednesday, I had just returned to my own house to change before dining with some friends, when I heard a commotion downstairs in the hall and a voice insistently demanding, 'Where is my nephew? Where is he? I will speak with him.'

There was no mistaking that voice and there was no mistaking the tone. My aunt, Lady Catherine de Bourgh, was most seriously displeased.

Although I could not imagine what quarrel my aunt had with me, I felt, for an instant, all the trepidation of a guilty schoolboy. A moment later, I was angry: angry because I had felt that way, angry that she was hectoring my servants, angry at this most acrimonious intrusion into my house.

Summoning to my assistance all that was left of my arrogance and disdain, I sauntered down the stairs, regarding the scene before my eyes with some disapprobation.

My aunt and my butler, being engaged in a battle of their own, were neither of them as yet aware of my presence. Monkton was politely insistent he had no idea whether or not his master was at home, but if her ladyship would be so obliging as to step into the blue saloon, he would endeavour to discover if I could be seen.

My aunt, incensed by what she correctly understood as my butler's intention to give me the opportunity of escape, was threatening him with all the dire consequences of displeasing a lady of her rank and importance.

'Do you know who I am?' she was demanding. 'Do you dare to trifle with me? I will not be thwarted. I will speak with him. Now, where is he?'

'He is here, madam,' I said. When she turned to look at me I favoured her with my most insolent bow and went on, 'To what do I owe the honour of this visit?'

'Does not your own conscience, sir, tell you why I come?' she said, to the interest of at least two of my servants.

'I am not aware you have any claims on my conscience at this present,' I replied coldly. 'And I might wish to know why you choose to impose such a claim upon me, here, in my own house and in presence of my servants? I do not care for such treatment, madam, and so I take leave to tell you.'

Such reproofs would not deflect my aunt from her purpose. She followed me into the blue saloon and there began again. 'Do not imagine, sir, that I am in ignorance concerning the upstart pretensions of Miss Elizabeth Bennet. She may have drawn you in by her allurements, but if you are sensible of your own good you will not forget what you owe to yourself and your family. I will remind you, sir, that you are engaged to my daughter.'

I know not whether I was the more astonished or embarrassed by the nature of my aunt's application. I could, however, easily comprehend how she had come by whatever information she had. I said grimly, 'I am, I take it, indebted to Mr Collins and his gossiping in-laws, the Lucases, for the pleasure of this visit. I am obliged to them!'

I had been leaning with my arm along the mantelpiece. Now, I drew myself up to my full height and turned to face my aunt. 'You choose to remind me, madam, of an engagement which you have proposed and which I have never acknowledged. Neither do I acknowledge it now. I do not consider myself bound to marry Anne.'

'You have known from your infancy that you were destined for your cousin! It was my favourite wish and that of your mother: we planned the union whilst you were in your cradles.'

'It is not my favourite wish, and you —'

'Silence! I will not be interrupted. You are formed for each other, you are destined for each other by every member of your respective houses. Are you to be divided now by the impertinent pretensions of a young woman of inferior birth, one without fortune or connection? This is not to be endured. I will not endure it. I have told Miss Bennet I shall carry my point, and I shall not be dissuaded from it. I shall not go away, sir, until you give me the assurance she refuses to give. I demand your promise that you will never enter into an engagement with Miss Bennet.'

'Madam—' I stopped as all the astonishing implications struck me at once. 'Am I to infer from this,' I spoke slowly and coldly, 'that with no better information than the idle gossip of the Lucases, you have been to Hertfordshire, to Longbourn, to importune Miss Bennet on the subject? You take too much upon yourself, madam. Indeed you do.'

'Am I not one of the nearest relations you have in the world?' she demanded. 'Am I not entitled to know all your concerns? She denies all knowledge of it, but mark my words, sir, I have no doubt the report of your attachment to Miss Bennet has been circulated by the lady herself.'

'I am sure it has not,' I said. Elizabeth, who had not even told her sister of our meeting in Derbyshire, could not be responsible for this. It was more likely some look or expression of mine had betrayed my sentiments to the Lucases when we all dined at Longbourn. 'And what did you propose, madam, what did you expect to achieve, by this excursion?'

'I hoped to find Miss Bennet reasonable as soon as I made my sentiments known to her. But I did not. She is obstinate and headstrong. She refuses to acknowledge the claims of your cousin; she refuses to have any regard for the wishes of your family and friends; she refuses to oblige me!'

'Indeed?' I could easily comprehend Elizabeth, offended by my aunt's manner and importunings, refusing to oblige her. I did not dare raise my hopes on this intelligence alone. 'And in what manner did you expect to find her so desirous of obliging you? Did you—forgive me, I wish to be quite clear on this point—what particular assurances did you demand from Miss Bennet?'

'She is not, at present, engaged to you. That much she has admitted. But she has no regard for honour, or duty, or gratitude. She would not promise never to enter into such an engagement. She is determined to have you!'

Whilst I was wondering how far I could trust this opinion, my aunt began insisting I should make the promise which Elizabeth would not make. Upon discovering I would not give a satisfactory answer, she was obliging enough to inform me of some things Elizabeth had said, believing, I suppose, that my indignation would be aroused against what she called Elizabeth's insolence.

'How far your nephew might approve of your interference in his affairs, I cannot tell; but you have certainly no right to concern yourself in mine.'

I could imagine Elizabeth speaking so, but there was little enough in that speech to tell me what I wanted to know. Wishing to hear more, I determined to annoy my aunt: I told her it was the answer she deserved.

I heard more:

'I am not to be intimidated by anything so wholly unreasonable . . . would my refusing to accept his hand, make him wish to bestow it on his cousin? . . . You have widely mistaken my character, if you think I can be worked on by persuasions such as these.'

In her indignation, my aunt continued to spill out other things Elizabeth had said. I listened very carefully indeed and it struck me there was ambiguity in every speech. Elizabeth was refusing to oblige my aunt, but her own wishes were well concealed.

'If there is no other objection to my marrying your nephew, I shall certainly not be kept from it by knowing that his mother and aunt wished him to marry Miss de Bourgh.'

There was no mention of those other objections which might keep Elizabeth from marrying me, but I was sensible of them, all the same.

My aunt was not. 'She is a selfish, unfeeling girl! She must know such a connection would disgrace you in the eyes of everybody.'

'I daresay you were so obliging as to inform her of it,' I said coldly.

She had, and Elizabeth had told her she would not trouble herself over the family, because the world in general would have more sense.

I had but little time to indulge my faint stirrings of hope, for my aunt, perhaps noticing I was better pleased than she was, now began to represent to me all the advantages of marriage with my cousin, informing me once again that it was expected by the family and had been my mother's dearest wish.

'It was not my father's dearest wish,' I said. 'I know he tried to dissuade you from this ambition. Neither are the rest of the family especially desirous of the match, whatever you choose to believe. I am sorry to be so blunt, but you leave me no alternative. Understand me now, madam, once and for all: you will not persuade me into marriage with my cousin. I have no inclination for it.'

My aunt was shocked and outraged. 'Do you refuse to hon-our the wishes of your sainted mother?'

'I doubt my mother would have insisted upon it. Even had she done so, I must go against the wishes of one parent, for my father wished it not at all.'

The reproaches of my aunt left me feeling very uncomfort-able, indeed, for she did not scruple to lay before me the charge that I was disappointing all my cousin's hopes and expectations of felicity. 'Are you so lost to all feelings of delicacy?' she de-manded.

'Madam, I see little delicacy in your soliciting my hand for your daughter, and still less in the methods you employ. You have encouraged my cousin in whatever expectations she has of me. I have not. If she is truly distressed, you must console her as best you can. You have my leave to tell her I would make an abominable husband.'

'I am astonished, sir, shocked and astonished to find you so obstinate. I had thought you more sensible of what was due to your position than to be taken in by the designing aspirations of one so far beneath you, in birth, in fortune, everything! Are you so infatuated with this girl that you cannot see where your duty lies?'

'It is not my duty to marry my cousin and I know that many attempts have been made to warn you of my decision on the matter, for it was made a long time ago, certainly long before I met Miss Bennet,' I said. 'Even had the lady agreed to oblige you, I would not change it.'

My aunt, however, continued to lay the blame for her own

failed plans on what she chose to call my infatuation for Elizabeth, which, in turn, had been created by her designing arts
and allurements. She reminded me of Elizabeth's connections,
told me the disgraceful facts of the patched-up marriage between Lydia and Wickham. She ended by threatening me: she
would see to it that Elizabeth was never accepted by the family. She would make sure Elizabeth was censured, slighted and
despised by everyone connected with me.

'No lady bearing the name of Mrs Darcy will be censured,
or slighted, or despised, madam. Certainly not at your instiga-
tion. You are not so high you can browbeat me.'

I had spoken very quietly, holding my rage in check, but
something must have shown in my face, for my aunt clearly
had second thoughts about delivering the rest of her invective.
She did not go so far as to back down, however. She merely
counselled me to think about what she had said, assured me
she had my welfare at heart, and expressed her own certainty
that I would, when I brought reason to bear upon the matter,
see it in a different light.

Such reason as I had, was, after my aunt left, employed in
wondering how far I dared to raise my hopes again.

I had no time for reflection, for my aunt had delayed me,
and I had a dinner engagement to keep. But all throughout
that evening, as I talked with my companions or listened to
the musical entertainment provided, part of my mind was
engaged with the extraordinary intelligence my aunt had
brought me.

Elizabeth had refused my aunt the assurance she would not

enter into an engagement with me. I could not wonder she had treated the application with such scorn.

Yet there were other ways of expressing scorn, ways more suited to the open and frank nature of Elizabeth's disposition. I found it quite astonishing that my aunt had heard nothing of that disapprobation and dislike which had been so forthrightly expressed last April and which, in all my later dealings with Elizabeth, had so frequently served as a check upon my hopes.

I could not be mistaken: had Elizabeth been wholly decided against me, she would have no scruple in explaining this to my aunt, possibly expressing whatever opinions she held of me, and her certainty of miserable prospects in store for any lady unwise enough to marry me.

Perhaps Elizabeth was not wholly decided against me, after all. But still I could not hope, for the memory of that last, unhappy evening at Longbourn was with me. Certain I was that Mrs Bennet's civility to me had a purpose. Her design had been to keep me separate from Elizabeth and I could see no reason for it unless she was honouring a request from the lady herself.

Which just shows how far my wits had gone a-begging, for it was not until later, much later, as I paced the floor of my bedchamber unable to sleep, that I eventually hit upon the real explanation. When I did, I was amazed at my own stupidity in not realizing it sooner.

Mrs Bennet had succeeded in her true design as well as in the one I had imputed to her. The lady had been concerned, but not for Elizabeth, all her contrivance had been for Jane: her intention had been to keep me out of Bingley's way.

Another review of our last two encounters at Longbourn taught me it was possible, just possible, that Elizabeth had not been displeased with me, as I had thought. We had, after all, been in company, unable to speak freely. I had felt awkward and embarrassed: perhaps she had felt the same way.

Another review of my aunt's visit now dared me to hope.

Tomorrow I would return to Netherfield: as soon as possible, I would contrive private speech with Elizabeth. My resolution was fixed: I was determined to know everything.

Seventeen

⸺❧⸺

WHEN I ARRIVED AT NETHERFIELD ON THE FOLLOW-
ing day, I was told Mr Bingley was at Longbourn and not expected back until late that evening. He returned eventually,
pleased to see me, and I spent an hour then listening to his
discourse on the perfections of his lady.

'Oh, Darcy,' he sighed, 'I wish you could be as happy. I
wish there was another Jane for you.'

'I thank you, but I think a less agreeable lady would suit me
better,' I said.

'Oh, Lord!' Bingley was at once conscience-stricken. 'Darcy, what was I thinking of? I would not for the world —'

'It is of no consequence,' I said. 'Have you spent all your
time at Longbourn whilst I have been away?'

'Most of it.' He went on to give me a description of Mrs

Bennet's ingenious stratagems to leave him alone with Jane so he could propose, most of which had been foiled by Elizabeth's determination to spare her sister's embarrassment. When Mrs Bennet had eventually won, he and Jane had laughed so much it was a wonder he had been able to declare himself at all.

He talked on, but told me nothing of what I wanted to know. Either he was ignorant of my aunt's visit to Longbourn or else he saw no significance in it, for it was not mentioned, even when I said I had seen Lady Catherine in town. I watched him carefully, but there was nothing in his expression to suggest he was concealing knowledge of it.

Elizabeth, I concluded, was still keeping her own affairs private, even from Jane.

Bingley was, quite understandably, far more interested in his own present situation than in my affairs. When I said I would accompany him to Longbourn the next day, it did not appear to cross his mind I had any design of my own.

Elizabeth looked a little pale, a little surprised to see me, but she quickly assumed her blank-faced expression and I could detect nothing of her feelings.

When Bingley proposed we should all walk out together, she agreed to it. Mrs Bennet was not much in the habit of walking; Mary Bennet declared she had to study; Catherine Bennet looked as though she wished she could think of an excuse to remain at home.

I also wished she could think of an excuse to remain at home. Clearly, Bingley intended to be alone with Jane and I was destined to accompany the other two ladies. Resigning myself to this, I hoped Catherine would somehow become detached from us, if only for a few minutes. Then, I could make a quiet request of Elizabeth for private conference at some later date.

Five of us set off together. Bingley and Jane soon lagged behind and although Catherine Bennet had been unable to find an excuse to stay at home, she quickly found an excuse to leave us. She requested we should walk in the direction of Lucas Lodge, saying she would like to call upon Maria Lucas, if we had no objection.

Elizabeth said she had no objection, neither did she express any desire to call upon the Lucases herself.

I said nothing. Elizabeth knew we were going to be alone together and if she had not contrived the situation, she had made no attempt to avoid it, either. She was uneasy, which troubled me, for I had perceived she had a purpose of her own.

I swallowed and braced myself, for if she had something to say to me, I could only assume it was to do with my aunt's ill-judged visit to Longbourn.

I was wrong: Elizabeth's mind was occupied with a very different matter, one so far removed from my own thoughts that I was quite startled to be reminded of it.

My attempt to conceal my part in arranging the marriage of her youngest sister to Wickham had been less successful than I thought.

'Mr Darcy,' she said, 'I can no longer help thanking you for your unexampled kindness to my poor sister. Ever since I have known it, I have been most anxious to acknowledge to you how gratefully I feel it. Were it known to the rest of my family, I should not have merely my own gratitude to express.'

There were tears in her eyes as she spoke and I felt an ache in my throat, for I realized she had been carrying this burden alone for some time. Never had it been my intention she should know of it and I said so, adding, rather sadly, 'I did not think Mrs Gardiner was so little to be trusted.'

'You must not blame my aunt,' she said quickly. 'Lydia's thoughtlessness first betrayed to me that you had been concerned in the matter, and, of course, I could not rest until I knew all the particulars.'

She resumed her thanks, on behalf of her family.

'If you *will* thank me,' I said, 'let it be for yourself alone. Your *family* owe me nothing. I thought only of *you*.'

Elizabeth looked away, pink with embarrassment, and I realized that I had, in a moment of uncomfortable emotion, unwittingly declared myself. Now, it was absolutely necessary to go on.

Quite forgetting the pretty proposal I had rehearsed, I simply begged her to tell me at once if her feelings were still the same as they were in April. '*My* affections and wishes are unchanged,' I added, 'but one word from you will silence me on this subject for ever.'

'I think you know,' she said, glancing at me and then away again, 'that my feelings are not at all what they were last April. How could they be, after everything that has happened, everything I have learnt? I think you know that . . . er . . . since that time . . . my feelings have changed . . . more than I would have . . . thought possible. . . .'

The rest of her reply descended into such incoherence that I could only catch the occasional word, but I understood what I was hearing: it was not what I had feared I must hear, but rather what I wished to hear.

Anxiety gave way to relief, relief brought with it all sweet sensations of happiness and I gazed at her in wonder and delight as I thanked her. I told her how beautiful she was, I told her all my love, my joy, my fervent intention to devote my life to ensuring her happiness. And she listened and blushed and smiled, but still she would not look at me.

We walked on, too busy with our own concerns to look around us. Having told her how my aunt's visit had restored me to hope, we fell to discussing the past. I told her how ashamed I had been, and still was, of my behaviour towards her; of how I understood how fully deserved her reproofs had been; of all the painful but valuable lessons I had taken from them.

And I learnt that upon reading my letter, she, that dear lady who had no cause for self-reproach whatever, had, nevertheless, reproached herself. She confessed she felt she had been foolish, blind and prejudiced and had, in her judgement of me, driven reason away.

We walked on. We talked of our meeting at Pemberley, and I told her how delighted Georgiana had been to know her and how disappointed when she had to leave Derbyshire so suddenly. We spoke again of the reasons for that departure, but I could see the subject still pained her and I quickly moved on to a happier topic: the engagement between Bingley and Jane.

'I must ask whether you were surprised?' said Elizabeth.

'Not at all. When I went away, I felt that it would soon happen.'

She nodded. 'That is to say, you had given your permission. I guessed as much.'

'My permission! He did not need—' I stopped, recalling how agitated Bingley had been when he was telling me he meant to go against what he thought were my wishes. I sighed. Perhaps Elizabeth was not so far wrong, after all.

I gave her a brief account of my talk with Bingley and it must have lost or gained something in the telling for Elizabeth seemed to be diverted by it.

'He will be happy,' I said, 'and so will your sister, for Bingley is the most amiable man. I am very much afraid,' I added, 'that of the two of you, your sister is getting the better husband.'

Elizabeth did not contradict me. 'Jane deserves it,' she said, 'for she has truly the sweetest nature of anyone I know. Would you believe she always refuses to think ill of anyone, even of you? Astonishing, I know, but so it is. So you see, your friend is wiser than you in his choice of wife.'

I smiled, knowing that Elizabeth, even in the worst of her humours, was far better suited to my own disposition. She would scold me, quarrel with me, torment me, tease me and laugh at me as often as may be.

I was the happiest man in the world.

We were late arriving back at Longbourn. We stayed apart, keeping our news to ourselves, for Elizabeth had expressed a desire to acquaint Jane privately with our situation before it became known to the rest of her family. The length of time we had been absent was remarked upon, but no one, not even Bingley, seemed to be at all suspicious.

The evening passed quietly. I noticed Mrs Bennet gazing fondly at Bingley and Jane. Nothing would ever give that lady wisdom, but I saw she was quieter, more sedate, now her worst fears had been laid to rest.

On the way back to Netherfield, I told Bingley that Elizabeth had consented to be my wife.

Bingley said the silliest thing. 'Oh, Darcy, are you sure?'

'I fully acknowledge,' I said, 'that I have made a fool of myself in fifty different ways: I am not, however, quite as delusional as that implies. Of course I am sure. Somehow, she has come to a better opinion of me. She loves me and we are engaged.'

He was incredulous, delighted, demanding to know every particular, and many hours of the night were spent in talk.

The warmth of Jane's smile as she greeted me the following morning left me in no doubt she was as pleased as Bingley had predicted she would be. Mrs Bennet, still desirous of getting me out of Bingley's way, proposed Elizabeth and I should walk out together, assuring me I would be most impressed with the view from Oakham Mount.

I meant to ask her father's consent that evening. Elizabeth looked a little uncomfortable when I suggested it and I smiled at her. 'Do not make yourself uneasy, my love. I know I am not a favourite with your parents: I shall know how to deal.'

'It is so unjust!' She was burning with anger. 'To treat you in so cavalier a fashion, when we owe you so much.'

'They know nothing of that,' I reminded her.

'Well, I do, and it pains me to see them making such a fuss of Bingley and yet treating you so coldly.'

I smiled at her, not minding in the least.

'I would feel easier if Papa was expecting it,' she said. 'But he has not the smallest suspicion. He received a letter from Mr Collins a few days ago. Can you guess what it said?'

'Something to the effect that Lady Catherine does not look upon our union with favour?' I suggested.

'Papa found it excessively diverting,' she said gloomily. 'He said the Lucases could not have hit upon a more absurd idea. He believes you have never looked at me in your life. So certain he was, I almost believed it myself.'

'I love you,' I said. 'Believe that: now we are come together, all other things are possible.'

It was Mr Bennet's habit to withdraw to his library soon after dinner: that evening, I followed him.

He was astonished to see who sought conference with him. 'Mr Darcy! I had not —' He rose from his chair. 'You wish to speak with me, sir?'

'Yes, sir.' I made my most respectful bow. 'I am to inform you, sir, that your daughter Elizabeth and I have formed an attachment for each other. We wish to be married, sir, and I come now to ask you to consent to our union.'

My application did not receive the most flattering of receptions. His initial astonishment gradually gave way to such dismay that the blood drained from his face. He sat down again and it was several minutes before he could speak.

I was sorry for him, for it was clear he had no idea what to make of it. I waited in silence, feeling that neither my sympathy nor assistance would be welcome in this extremity.

Recovering at last, he invited me to sit and then said, 'You must forgive me, Mr Darcy. I had no idea of such attachment. We have seen but little of you at Longbourn. I confess I am at a loss to understand how it has come about.'

'Elizabeth and I have seen more of each other than you might suppose, sir. We met in Kent during the spring and we met again when she was in Derbyshire with Mr and Mrs Gardiner.'

He had nodded when I mentioned Kent, although I knew he had never been informed of what took place there. He was a little taken aback to learn of Derbyshire. I went on, 'We have come to know each other well enough to be certain of our feelings.'

He blinked rapidly once or twice. He would not say she disliked me but he thought it. He attributed to Elizabeth another motive for accepting my proposals.

I said coolly, 'Do not imagine, sir, I am ignorant of how much Elizabeth disliked me, at first. She had reason, though perhaps not as much reason as she thought.'

He was surprised but did not deny she had ever thought ill of me. He remained silent, thinking it over. At last, he said, 'So you believe she now has a better opinion of you?'

'I do,' I said firmly. He continued to look unconvinced and unhappy, and I added, 'I believe you will, if you reflect upon the matter, recall that you have heard nothing from Elizabeth on the subject for some time now.'

'Perhaps you are right.' At this point Mr Bennet seemed to remember I might feel somewhat affronted to have my very flattering proposals treated with so little enthusiasm. In the eyes of the world I was, after all, a most eligible suitor. 'Now you come to mention it, I believe you are right.' He strove manfully to account for his initial dismay by saying he had not expected to lose his favourite daughter so soon.

He gave his consent: he had no just reason for refusing it. He tried to look happy about it and I assured him I had a very sincere regard for his daughter. I said I understood his reservations and suggested he should talk to Elizabeth.

He would, I knew, try to talk her out of it. Certain as I was he would not succeed, the next hour was painful to me for I knew those two were making each other unhappy. It was a relief to see her looking tolerably composed when she returned to the drawing-room. Her smile convinced me she had gone some way towards reconciling her father to the match.

The next day, Mr Bennet sought me out, embarrassed now, because Elizabeth had told him I made up the match between Lydia and Wickham. It took some time to convince him neither his thanks nor his offer of repayment was necessary, but he gave way in the end, knowing my actions had been governed by a desire to spare Elizabeth's distress.

'I confess I am relieved to discover I am not indebted to my brother Gardiner,' he said. 'My greatest fear was that he had distressed himself to bring it about.'

I had a minor triumph later that day, and I confess I was mean enough to enjoy it. For Elizabeth told me, that upon informing her mother of our engagement, Mrs Bennet had been wholly still and wholly silent for a full fifteen minutes.

All Mrs Bennet's dislike of me was done away with at a stroke. There are cynics who will say my wealth and consequence must account for this, and I have no doubt it played a part, as did the fact of her social triumph in wedding one of her daughters to such an illustrious personage as myself. But I understood that lady a little better, now. Her understanding was weak; she was always foolish, always imprudent and very often an embarrassment. She was also fiercely partial towards her own daughters. It was my displaying such excellent taste and good sense as to wish to marry one of them which really secured her favour.

It was Mrs Bennet who proposed the scheme which brought me to matrimony sooner than I expected, for, having become engaged whilst the arrangements for Bingley's wedding to Jane were underway, I had been resigned to the idea of waiting for some time before our own wedding could be arranged.

'No, no, my dears,' said Mrs Bennet. 'You must have a double wedding. Between such close sisters and such close friends, there can be no possible objection. Yes, yes! You must apply straight away for a special licence. A double wedding! It will be of all things most charming.'

I wish I could say that my aunt, Lady Catherine, was reconciled to our engagement. She was not, however, and I will not repeat what she said in her letter to me. It is enough to say I was resolved to have nothing more to do with her.

The first letter from my cousin, Colonel Fitzwilliam, consisted of only two words: it said simply: 'At last!' A second letter, arriving the next day, expressed his congratulations in a more seemly way.

The other Fitzwilliams, contrary to the expectations of my aunt, wrote to say they were happy for me; they had heard much of Elizabeth and were most eager to make her acquaintance.

Georgiana was delighted. She had been shy when talking to Elizabeth, but she had no reserve when expressing herself in writing and her letter to Elizabeth ran to four pages, leaving no one in doubt of her sentiments.

I received an equally warm letter of congratulations from Mr and Mrs Gardiner.

As our engagement became generally known, Elizabeth and I found ourselves constantly separated by the attentions of other people.

Mr Bennet invited me to go shooting with him, a clear indication he was exerting himself to get to know me better. It was a day well spent, for we found we had much in common in our knowledge of the countryside and in our interest in books, and when I invited him to visit Pemberley and inspect the library there, he looked much happier about losing his favourite daughter. What he said to Elizabeth later, I know not, but I could see by the warmth of her smile that it pleased her.

Mr and Mrs Collins appeared in the neighbourhood. Anxious to escape the wrath of my aunt, they had come to stay at Lucas Lodge until it subsided. For Elizabeth there was pleasure in having her friend with her, and I, mindful that Mr Collins had played his part in securing my present happiness, found within myself more patience with the gentleman than I had expected.

Mr Bennet, observing this, told me I was in serious danger of getting a good name for myself.

Sir William Lucas complimented me, more than once, on carrying away the brightest jewel of the country, and spoke of a future in which he hoped we would all meet frequently at St James's Court. I knew he had said exactly the same to Bingley.

Mrs Bennet and her sister Mrs Philips were deep in all those mysterious details so necessary to the proper arrangement of elegant nuptials. Elizabeth and Jane were frequently called into conference with them to discuss all the particulars of silk and satin and lace. Jane bore it all with unfailing patience; Elizabeth was heard to mutter that perhaps an elopement was not such a dreadful idea, after all.

For myself I was contented enough, knowing there were but a few days now before we took our vows and we would be left alone afterwards. It did not escape my notice, however, that Elizabeth was growing fretful and every time I tried to discover the reason, someone came along to consult with one or the other of us on some matter needing immediate attention.

Mr Collins was the worst offender, for his discourse upon even the most trivial matter seemed to take a most complicated route before reaching its conclusion. Mrs Collins eventually rescued me, finding some matter requiring her husband's attention. Then, without ceremony, she pushed me into the deserted dining-room and told me to stay there.

'I have sent Lizzy upstairs to change,' she said. 'It is a fine day and I advise you, sir, to take her out for a nice long walk. And do not go in the direction of Meryton, for there you are bound to meet someone you know. All this fuss is really too much for Lizzy: she needs a little respite. And so do you, unless I am very much mistaken. So go, and do not return until dinner-time. The rest of us can spare you for a few hours, I am sure.'

Elizabeth and I sidled away from Longbourn like two children playing truant. She walked a little ahead of me, her face flushed, her mouth set in a straight line of temper.

I said nothing. If, as Mrs Collins had indicated, it was only the press of people troubling her, she would laugh herself out of her ill-humour sooner for being left alone.

As, indeed, she did. She then had a little to say about the absurdities we had both endured and unwittingly relieved my own fears when she said, 'I confess, they have greatly taxed my forbearance. How I look forward to the time when we can be removed from company, and be quiet and comfortable together.'

The lightening of my heart must have shown in my expression for she looked enquiry at me. 'I have been troubled, I own, in case you were regretting your decision to marry me.'

'No, indeed, nothing like that,' she said simply.

There it was, that look for which I had once said I would sacrifice my right arm. It would have been a small price to pay, too. But no such sacrifice was required, and I was glad, for I had found a good use for my right arm. I slipped it round her shoulders, drew her towards me, and bent my head to claim her mouth with my own.

I bungled it.

Somehow, our noses bumped, my mouth touched her chin and slid away to nothing. Embarrassed, furious with myself, I turned away from her, hunching my shoulders moodily, unable to bear myself for being so clumsy.

There was a silence. Then I heard a faint gurgle of laughter and her voice, when it came, spoke with strong, authoritative tones in a fair imitation of my aunt, Lady Catherine.

'You will never kiss really well, Mr Darcy,' she said, 'unless you practise more. You cannot expect to excel if you do not practise a great deal.'

Advice which, I felt, contained some good, solid reasoning and sound common sense. I turned back to her with a rather sheepish smile. 'I assure you, madam,' I said, 'that from now on, I intend to practise very constantly.'

I suited my action to my words. And if the first kiss had gone something awry, the second was most satisfactory in every particular.